# BOOKS BY KRISTIE COOK

### Soul Savers

Recommended Reading Order:

A Demon's Promise

An Angel's Purpose

Genesis: A Soul Savers Novella

Dangerous Devotion

Dark Power

Sacred Wrath

Unholy Torment

Fractured Faith

Age of Angels Part I: Awakened

Age of Angels Part II: Lost

Age of Angels Part III: Marked

Prophecy of the Wolves: (A Soul Savers Tie-In Novella)

Wonder: A Soul Savers Collection of Holiday Short Stories & Recipes

### Knights of Souls and Shadows

Knights of Souls and Shadows, Book 1

### Havenwood Falls

Recommended Reading Order:

Forget You Not

Lose You Not

Break Me Not

The Collector: Awakening

Savage Salvation (Sin & Silk)

Sun & Moon Academy Book One: Fall Semester

Sun & Moon Academy Book Two: Fall Semester

The Winged & the Wicked (with T.V. Hahn)

Havenwood Falls Short Story Anthology 2018

Havenwood Falls Short Story Anthology 2019

Havenwood Falls Short Story Anthology 2020

**BOOK OF PHOENIX**

The Space Between

The Space Beyond

The Space Within

SOUL SAVERS BOOK 10

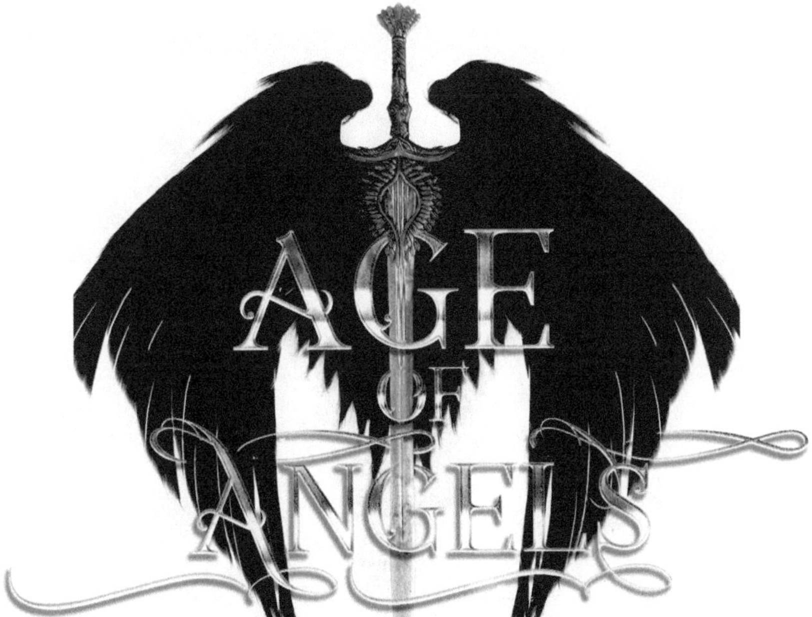

# AGE OF ANGELS

## PART III: MARKED

### KRISTIE COOK

*To the Crazy Aunts*
*You Know Who You Are*

# PROLOGUE

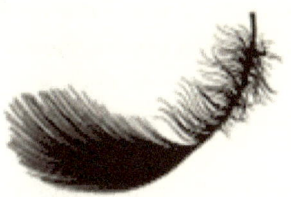

S creams pierce the air from every direction, the roar of the
tornadic wind doing its best to drown them out. Long spears of
ice pelt down, stabbing into the ground like frozen, deadly daggers. A
building on the town square bursts into flames as another explodes,
blasting out a dangerous cloud of glass shards, brick chunks, and wood
splinters that shower over half the town. The ground quakes and rumbles,
and I watch with horror as cracks carve into the road and across the
mayor's dusty lawn. Bodies litter the ground, and I pray they still hold
life.

For at the center of it all, hovering in the air as the tornado churns
around them—the very creators of the tornado itself and all of the other
destructive forces—are my twin daughters.

Ten minutes ago, they'd been sound asleep in Scout's spare bedroom
at her house in the small town of Ravenbury. Barely more than an hour
ago, they'd returned from wherever they'd been for the last couple of
months—lost from us, from this world, but where, we still had no idea.
They'd passed out moments after appearing here in Ravenbury, seemingly
out of nowhere, and Scout had taken them in. They'd only awaken long
enough for Elliana to share a secret she'd been keeping before passing out
again.

Then Ranker—the mayor of Misery's Edge, a trading town nearly two
hundred miles from here—showed up with his men, to arrest me for
murder.

I don't know if that was the spark that ignited their fury or something else happened, but suddenly my daughters, who'd never been able to flash before, appeared in the middle of the street, between Ranker's group and me. Their wings, purple and black like mine, rose majestically behind them—the first time we'd seen them since the twins were a few days old. And they didn't burst from their backs in a shocking reveal, but simply appeared as though at will, just as their father and I could do. As if they'd done this a hundred times, which became more apparent when they used them expertly to lift into the air.

And then they unleashed their powers—powers they didn't have two months ago.

They easily took down Ranker and his group, including the mage he'd brought. And then anyone else who tried to stop them, even Tristan and me.

They ignored the pleas we shouted at them to stop. They blocked my telepathic ones, too. They'd shielded themselves against Owen's spells, and Tristan couldn't even paralyze them.

They were so damn powerful.

It was quite obvious they'd learned to use those powers, too. How? Where the hell had they been? Who taught them this? Had they been whisked away somewhere with the Angels to go through the Ang'dora? Without me? No, that wasn't right, because there was something else different about them, and not just that their hair was no longer a copper color like mine, but a black so dark it was almost blue.

We'd been warned that a darkness called to them, that their blood drew it to them, and we'd sensed a touch of dark energy surrounding them while they slept—but nothing like we'd been told to expect. Nothing some Amadis power couldn't counteract.

Or so I'd thought.

I needed to figure out how to stop them before they destroyed the entire town—killed any innocent people. Or, at least, any more than they might already had done.

At first, I thought they couldn't control their powers, their fingers twitching and jumping seemingly at random. But then I realized they were in perfect control—they were directing the power where they wanted it to go, to anyone who moved, especially in their direction. There was something in their eyes, though, that told me they didn't lack control, but they did lack awareness.

They were physically here, but mentally they were not. They didn't see or hear their parents trying to stop them. They didn't see or hear innocent townspeople simply trying to take cover or care for their wounded. They were somewhere else that was scaring the living shit out of them, and they were only trying to protect themselves.

"*What do we do?*" I mentally cried out to Tristan.

Before he could answer, a streak of motion soared down the road from the edge of town, right for us. Right for my girls. It paused long enough behind Brielle for me to see hands grasp her head and twist. Before I could even scream, it blurred to Elliana and snapped her neck, too.

My daughters' bodies—my *babies*—dropped in lifeless heaps on the ground.

And wearing a dark suit, his hands shoved into his pants pockets and Sasha at his feet, my son stood between them.

"Dorian!" I screamed, flying at him in a fit of rage.

He stopped me with a flick of his hand. He did the same to his father. We were held in place, though not completely paralyzed.

The tornado had stopped, dirt and bricks and other debris falling heavily to the ground. Everything became completely silent, as though a switch had been flipped, except for the sounds of weeping in the distance and fire crackling in the background.

"Hello, Mother, Father," Dorian greeted, his deep voice sounding almost bored. With the same tall and broad build as his father, the same hazel eyes and sandy brown hair, too, although Dorian's was cut short to his head, he could have been Tristan's twin. Except for the red glow in the backs of his eyes, barely noticeable now but I'd seen it before—the last time I'd seen him.

"What did you do?" I gasped.

"Sasha found me. Apparently, you needed help."

My brows furrowed, my brain not comprehending. I didn't give a shit about the *lykora* right now.

"WHAT DID YOU DO?" I screamed.

"I stopped them," he replied, his own voice calm and indifferent, almost cold, as if the bodies of his own sisters didn't lie at his feet. Still. Lifeless.

I blinked in disbelief, my heart cracking as my gaze dropped to their forms. I stared at my daughters' inert bodies, unable to breathe. Unable to think. All I could do was feel—feel the pain ripping through me, tearing out a piece of me. A large chunk—two large chunks of my heart and my soul. I tried again to go to them, but Dorian still held me in place. I couldn't break free of his power. Like his sisters, he was more powerful than we were.

"Just let me hold them!" I screamed as my body began to tremble.

*They're not dead. They cannot be dead. Not my daughters. No, no, no. Not my babies.* My head shook in denial. *This did not just happen.*

I'd heard all the stories about my son—the horrible, awful deeds he'd supposedly done. I could never believe them. Never accept them. I chose to ignore them, knowing my son could never be capable of such atrocities. But here we were—he'd just killed his own sisters.

"They can't be dead," I whispered out loud. "Please—"

"Oh, but they are," Dorian said, and a sob escaped my throat in a feral sound. "And they are not."

My gaze whipped up as my breath caught. Anger exploded in my chest. I gritted out my words. "What does that mean?"

At the same time, Tristan exploded. "What the *fuck* does that mean?"

Dorian simply shrugged. "We are the products of the Angels and the Demons, of vampires and shifters and sorcerers and fae. We are the offspring of you, the two most powerful creatures this world has ever known—until now, until us. Do you really think we can be killed so easily?"

# CHAPTER 1

*TWO YEARS LATER*

*M*y boots balance on the edge of the turbine's stationary blade as my wings hold me steady high above the town of Ravenbury. The townspeople go about their day, finishing up chores as the sun lowers in the western sky, casting that golden glow over the lands. Many people filter down the streets from the farms and crops on the edge of town, done with their work for the day. They aren't much—the farms and crops. The lands and the air and the waters still aren't back to normal. But Scout, the mayor, and her people have been able to protect enough of their crops and livestock to keep the town's residents from starving for this long. Hopefully, their situation will improve if we can get this turbine going and producing power again.

"Ready, Mom?" Brielle calls from below, her father by her side. She looks up at me with excited anticipation in her dark eyes, her black hair hanging down her back in a simple braid that's caught between the collar of her red flannel shirt and the tank she wears under it. The tank, her black leather pants, and boots are enchanted fighting gear. The flannel is a statement—particularly to her twin—that she couldn't care less what she wears or how she looks, a total affront to Elliana.

My gaze swings out over the town, looking for my other daughter but not seeing her, as I reply to Brielle and Tristan. "Ready!"

I fly up to the next highest blade and grasp the top edge with both hands. If not for my wings, it probably appears as though I'm hanging from the blade, my legs dangling as I wait for the word. Tristan's sandy-brown head bends closely to his daughter's dark one as they make some last-minute adjustments to the contraption they've been working on for weeks. When he looks up at me with those stunning hazel eyes, I can't help but smile. We've been together for how long now? And he still takes my breath away. Especially when he returns my smile and winks.

"Okay, Mom, do it!" Brielle yells, bouncing on the balls of her feet with excitement.

With all of my supernatural strength, I shove on the blade. It doesn't budge at first, and I think they might need to apply more lubrication to the rotor—or whatever they need to do, I confess to not understanding any of it, or really trying to understand, to be honest, because that's their thing—but then I feel a slight movement. Using my wings and all my weight as leverage, I push harder, and ever so slowly, the blades begin to move. I quickly fly out of the way, then fan the air, creating the wind to get it going.

Brielle whoops with glee from below.

Then we all watch, perfectly still with bated breath for a long, drawn-out moment, before lights flicker on one by one, illuminating windows in the falling dusk. Cheers start echoing from the residents. The town has been without power for several weeks, when a particularly bad electrical storm shut down the turbine and all of its components. With a mix of science and magic—our go-to solution anymore—Tristan, Brielle, and a small team had worked diligently to fix each piece in the chain that brings electricity to the town's homes and businesses. Until now, though, they haven't been able to get the blades themselves to turn, as though they'd been frozen or welded in place by the magical effects of that last storm. It's all more complex than I choose to give the time to figure out, so I've stayed out of most of it until now. When Brielle said this morning at breakfast that she had an idea for how to break the seal on the blades and she asked me to help, of course I couldn't say no.

This is one of the many ways my family has been making reparations to the town of Ravenbury over the last two years. Of course, only a few of us even know why—Tristan, me, and a few of my council members. Memories had been altered or even completely wiped, for the sake of keeping the peace and safety of all involved. At least, that's what I say to try to convince myself that it was the right thing to do. Guilt still sits heavily in my gut and keeps me awake at night, even when I know it was probably the best solution for the greater good.

I drop down and give my daughter a huge hug. "Congratulations, sweet girl, you did it!"

Something flickers in her eyes just briefly before her mouth stretches in a grin and those eyes light up. "We all did it. Each one of the team did their part to make this happen."

She doesn't like being called "sweet"—neither of the girls do, and not because it's embarrassing. Although they usually block me from telepathically entering their minds, I occasionally grasp tidbits that tell me they think of themselves far from sweet. Though they can't remember where they'd been in those months when they'd disappeared or what happened to them then and when they returned, they continue to harbor that thread of dark energy that is anything but sweet. They've each mentioned it to me on a few occasions—that difference they feel to everyone else, a sense of not quite belonging, an understanding that somewhere within them, buried deeply by powerful spells, slumbers a great and potentially world-destroying dark force.

To me, though, they will always be my sweet daughters. No, they're not perfect, and they're typical teenaged girls in many ways, but they aren't the monsters we'd been warned they could become. I refuse to believe my son is, either, despite his own claim and all of the evidence that continues to stack up against him. A monster doesn't go out of its way to protect anyone else, not even its family and especially not strangers in a town it knows nothing about or cares nothing for. Dorian did all of those, although his means left something to be desired.

Brielle, Tristan, and I stride down the street into the town's center to join everyone who's celebrating in the square.

"You're staying for dinner," Scout says as she falls in to step with us, her long legs more in sync with Tristan's than mine and Brielle's. She's tall, closer in height to him, and slender but strong for a human, even at her age, with reddish gray curls that bounce on her shoulders as she walks. She doesn't make it a question, and from her commanding presence, it's almost an order.

"Actually, we were just going to get the others and head back to The Loft," I say as we near the square where tables are already set up and food is being brought to fill them. While it looks like a spread worthy of a holiday feast, I know it's barely enough to feed the people of the town.

"But you're the guests of honor," Scout protests. "Especially Brielle here. Well, and Tristan gets a little credit." She winks at Brielle, who can't stop smiling.

"I just hope it lasts this time," she says, an edge of doubt in her tone.

My little engineer is bound and determined to figure out how to make electricity and magic cooperate once and for all so we can eventually bring technology back to our world. She's always been fascinated by the stories Tristan tells her about the gadgets of convenience we had in the Before time—toys, as he'd called them. Sure there are some still around, so she knows the truth in his stories, but they rarely work, and those that even turn on have little use when there's no internet or even a power grid to plug into. Every time progress is made with the power grids, a new storm whips up, some other natural disaster destroys it, or black magic fries it, setting us back again and again. It's the main reason the world seems to be stuck in a holding pattern all these years. Some claim Mother Earth doesn't want to take us back to the Before time, when humanity was virtually destroying her, but I can't imagine she likes what's here now.

No, it's not Mother Earth holding us back. It's the long-term effects of the nuclear and black magic bombs exacerbated by the blanket of dark energy that's been seeping into our world for years. In fact, although the gate the girls opened is sealed and cloaked, I swear the energy is similar as it continues to grow thicker and darker. That scares me a lot more than anything my daughters might do—but especially if it finds them, becomes them, as we'd been warned.

I shake the dismal thoughts off and return to the moment. "Even if it doesn't last, you know more now than you did a month ago. You'll be faster and better next time."

Brielle snorts. "If it was that easy, we'd be a lot further along by now. Every storm, every force that knocks it out each time is different, though, causing new problems."

"Well, eventually you'll have learned them all," Scout says, "and then nothing will stop you. I have full confidence that you will do amazing things for this world, Brielle. You and your sister both."

Once again, that gut-piercing guilt shoots through me.

Scout doesn't remember what my daughters did to her town, to her people. She should be afraid of them. She should be banning any of us from ever entering her borders again. But here she is, unaware and instead complimenting them, boosting Brielle's confidence, believing that they have a future of nothing but good. Which I so very much want to believe myself. It's probably why I shove away that guilt and the memories, so I can share Scout's optimism and belief in my girls' potential.

"While you're figuring out how to improve the world and everyone's lives, Elli will be saving it hunting Demons and other evil," I say.

Brielle gasps and looks at me with wide eyes. "You're going to let her join your elite team?"

Yeah, right. Not for at least ten more years, if I have my way. Not that Elliana isn't showing huge potential in that area. She's wanted to hunt and kill Demons since she was little. That's the one thing we know about that day they disappeared, when Charleigh finally admitted to her parents that they'd seen a Demon and Elli chased after it, the other two following her far beyond the boundaries of safety around The Loft.

"I'm sure she'll find a way to convince me one of these days," I reply, but my heart twists at the thought. While I know she'd be an excellent addition to my elite team, she's still my little girl. Unfortunately, Ragan, the human Demon hunter and leader of said team, has been begging me for more supernaturals to join her and knows there's nobody better than Elliana.

"Speaking of your sister, it looks like Elliana's made a new friend," Tristan says.

I follow his gaze to our other daughter, who's just sitting down at one of the tables with a young woman who looks around twenty or so and an elderly man I've never seen before. My jaw nearly drops open—Elliana *wants* to be a social butterfly, but she doesn't exactly give off the friendliest of vibes, especially to strangers. In fact, she can be downright intimidating. This is good, though, I think, seeing her befriend someone. This is progress.

She must have heard her father say her name, because she looks at us and waves, gesturing for us to come over.

"That's Daniela and her father Miguel," Scout says. "Vanny-Sue found them wandering in the canyon over yonder a few nights ago, starving and dehydrated, so she brought them here to rest."

Although the people of Ravenbury have no issues with the supernatural and they've been appreciative of all we've done for them in the past, everyone here is human—except for maybe Vanny-Sue. Blossom and I are sure she's a closet-witch. With silver hair that reaches her knees, Vanny-Sue is the oldest Ravenbury resident, but she's as tenacious as my Elli and full of knowledge about natural remedies and such. It's not uncommon for her to be roaming out in the wild at night, especially under a full moon. She has no fear of all that's out there, which only reinforces our belief that she has some kind of connection to magic—something she can use as a defense because her tiny, elderly frame would be zombie food in an instant.

"They've been traveling since the girl was seven years old," Scout continues. "As soon as they realized the area around them was safe, they left their shelter, coming all the way from a small town in Brazil."

I notice immediately that the newcomers are normal humans—what we call norms or Normans—which means they've been traveling on foot from that far. "Wow. Why?"

"They've been searching for someone Miguel knows."

"All this time?" Brielle asks.

"I guess it's someone special to him," Scout replies with a shrug. "He only knows a few words of English, so Dani does all the talking. She said they started with a big group, but it's dwindled over the years. Now it's just the two of them. He's such a sweet old man. I hope he finds who he's looking for before it's too late."

We go over to meet the pair and gather Elliana so we can head home, but before I know it, we're all sitting down and enjoying a meal together. Tristan, the man of many tongues, speaks easily with Miguel in Brazilian Portuguese. Picking up on a few words here and there and filling the rest in with their thoughts, I'm able to follow along. Scout's right—Miguel is a sweetheart and full of interesting and entertaining stories of the Before time and of their travels. The poor man has obviously missed good conversation with another person besides his daughter, who's probably heard these stories a hundred times—the ones she hasn't lived through herself. With each one, I'm more amazed that they've made it so far.

As Miguel talks, though, I don't miss the connection Elli has made with Daniela. They seem to be in their own world, tuning out the rest of us, to the point that Elliana jumps when Charleigh bounds up behind her. Elli is rarely caught off guard, her senses always fully in tune with everything going on around her—that's been her training ever since the girls were young but especially in the past two years.

"Elli, we still have a few more things to finish up," Charleigh says as she drops a hand on Elli's shoulder. Dani's gaze lingers on it before swinging up to the girls' best friend and cousin, by choice if not by blood. She takes in Charleigh's orange hair that flows well past her shoulders and her eyes that are such a strange brown, they're almost as orange as her hair, especially when she's angry, which she isn't now. She's curious, though, eyeing the stranger back. Dani gives a faint smile as they're introduced, but immediately turns her attention back to Elli, as though waiting to see if she'll be leaving her side. I stay out of all of their minds, granting them privacy, but wonder what kind of dynamics seem to be already forming.

"Um—" Elli looks at Dani, not even turning to see Charleigh behind her.

Brielle jumps to her feet next to me. "I can help."

Charleigh's brows pinch as she studies Elli, then she nods before looking at me. "We're almost done, Aunt Alexis. Mom says no more than another hour or so."

"Okay. We'll find you in a bit."

The girls hurry off toward the town's apothecary, leaving Elli with Dani. Blossom, Charleigh, and Elliana had been working with Vanny-Sue on restocking the apothecary's shelves with healing potions, tinctures, and herbs earlier while we'd been working on the turbine.

"Elli, don't you think you should help your aunt?" I ask her.

"Brie—"

"Brie already helped turn the power back on. Are you going to let her do your job, too?"

Elli frowns, but Dani speaks up, her accent thick but her English perfect. "I can help, too. We'll get it done faster that way."

"Sure, okay," Elli quickly agrees, standing. Her words float over her shoulder as she turns to follow her sister and best friend. "Brie is perfectly happy and capable to do it, but obviously, my mom will never let this go."

I snort as I watch them walk away, and when their arms brush against each other's a couple of times, I immediately realize what Brie already knows—there's something more than friendship sparking between Elliana and the newcomer. An inexplicable fear seizes my heart. I don't know why. I want nothing more than for my daughter to be happy, and it's not exactly easy for a queer girl to find love in our world, especially when we've had to keep her pretty isolated from other people. I can only figure it's the other girl's age—because she's not exactly a girl. She's twenty-one, three years older than Elli and with a lot more life experience, considering she's traveled across entire continents and endured many hardships my daughters have been blessed to never experience. I can't possibly know how many others Dani might have been with in the past, none or many, but I do know this is a relationship that can't last. My own heart is already cracking for the heartbreak Elli will inevitably suffer, probably sooner than later.

Trying to ignore the need to protect her by inserting myself now, I turn my attention back to Miguel and Tristan.

Tristan lays an arm over my shoulder. "He says he's very impressed by our daughters."

"Oh, really?" I ask.

Miguel's shaggy salt-and-pepper hair brushes over his shirt collar as he nods enthusiastically. His gray mustache and thick brows contrast against his deep golden skin and dark eyes, which sparkle with a heart-melting grin. "*Muito esperto.*"

"Very smart," Tristan translates.

"I can't argue with that," I say, and add, "sometimes more than what's good for them or the rest of us."

The older man laughs after Tristan translates again.

"He understands," Tristan says. "He says Dani is the same, always keeping him on his toes."

Miguel says something more.

"She's taken good care of him, though," Tristan says. "He doesn't know what he would do without her."

"I die," Miguel says, placing his closed fist against his chest. "Broken heart. She ... my world."

I nod. "I understand. It's hard being a parent, isn't it? Even when they grow up?"

He laughs, crinkles spreading out from the corners of his eyes. "*Muito.*"

He continues, then Tristan translates. "He says *especially* when they grow up. They're like a piece of your heart walking around and eventually we have to let them go."

I suck in my bottom lip to bite it, driving away the threatening tears at this truth. Miguel doesn't miss a thing, reaching out to take my hand.

"*É bom,*" he says. "It good. Be okay."

I turn my hand over to squeeze his as I nod. "You're right. It's how life is supposed to be."

But not yet. I refuse to let them go yet.

Tristan and I eventually say our goodbyes to Miguel and stand to find the rest of our people.

A few minutes later, we all gather in front of the apothecary, ready to head back to The Loft.

"Wait," I say, glancing around. "Where's Elliana?"

We all turn our attention to Charleigh and Brielle. Brie just shrugs.

Charleigh finally answers, her voice smaller and quieter than usual. "We, uh, can't find her anywhere."

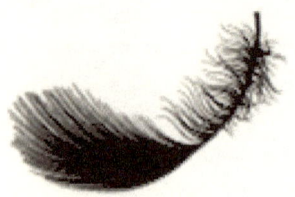

# CHAPTER 2

*I*'m instantly taken back to two years ago, when she'd told me the girls had disappeared. It's irrational, of course. I know the panic that's gripping my soul and seizing my lungs is completely ridiculous. The situation is totally different. Not only is Brielle still here and fine, but neither she nor Charleigh is in the least bit scared or worried. Maybe a little concerned mixed with some guilt—I can sense both from them.

But still, my mind immediately goes to those moments in the past when we'd lost the girls and imagines Elli out there in the wilderness between here and home, with the zombies and Demons and of course the dragons, who I don't think will hurt her, not on purpose anyway, and then there's whatever had taken them before, or swallowed them or whatever had happened that we still don't fully know and Dorian wouldn't explain—

"Alexis," Tristan says, interrupting my thoughts and stopping the runaway train in my mind. "Find her."

I blink, then mentally give myself a shake before reaching out with my telepathy. But my brows tighten. "I can't. She's either gone or completely closed me off. Who saw her last?"

"That would be me," Blossom says, gathering her long blond hair over her shoulder and twisting it in her hands. "We needed some more jars, and Vanny-Sue had mentioned earlier that there might be a few out at Scout's farmhouse. I thought it would be safe."

Scout's family farm sits south of town, not even a quarter-mile from the town's border. When she was elected mayor after the war, she moved into a house near the square to be closer to everyone, so the farmhouse sits vacant of people, but not empty.

"I told her to go, that she needs to do her share," Brielle adds, and now I understand the guilt. "Dani went with her."

"But we couldn't find them there," Charleigh finishes.

"Dani's Norman," I say as I press my hand against my forehead. "If there were any zombies or Demons out there, Elli would have been fighting them by herself." I don't even want to consider that she might have disappeared once again, but a small part of my mind goes there anyway—thus the fear and panic pushing at my lungs, my heart.

"Dani survived a long time in the wild," Tristan reminds me. "I'm sure she can hold her own."

"I don't care. We need to find them!"

Within minutes, we're pairing off to search, and that irrational fear threatens to explode. We really don't know anything about this Dani except for the stories Miguel told us. As sweet as he seems, maybe there's more to them. Maybe they're not what they appear to be, but are big Trouble with a capital T. Maybe that's what I really sensed earlier from the woman who was making googly eyes at my barely-of-age daughter—not that she'd break Elli's heart, but worse.

How could we be so stupid? A tingle pricks the back of my neck as I recall the warnings we'd been given, particularly that of other factions wanting to use my daughters, or to kill them. We'd kept them hidden and safe so far, cloaked from everyone except those at The Loft and here in Ravenbury. One of the secret reparations we'd made for Scout and her people was to magically protect the town from being discovered by nefarious wanderers and travelers. But Dani and Miguel hadn't found the town—they'd been brought here.

I take to the sky, sending my senses out, monitoring all of the mind signatures as I fly to the south, toward Scout's farmhouse. I don't find Elli's, but I do pick up on the new one—Dani's—in a barn another half-mile past the house. As I close in both physically and mentally, I finally grasp onto Elli's mind signature, though I can't break through her mental shield. I've noticed she's become better and better at blocking me, but this is the first time she's hidden her mind so thoroughly. Or has Dani somehow been able to do it?

I telepathically alert the others as I drop to the ground in front of the barn, where huge but faded letters span the broadside, warning "THE END IS NEAR" but someone crossed out "NEAR" and wrote in "HERE." Tristan and Brielle land to each side of me just before Elli rushes out of the door, her hands tugging at the hem of her top as her dark gaze sweeps over us but never really *looks* at us.

"Uh, sorry," she says, glancing at me for the briefest moment before her attention darts to her sister.

Out of the corner of my eye, I see Brielle gesturing at the side of her head. Elli's own hand flies to her hair, picking out a piece of straw and smoothing down her uncharacteristically messy locks, all the while giving me a falsely innocent look. Her tongue sweeps over puffy lips, and when Dani follows behind, I notice her hair is just as disheveled and her lips are swollen, too.

Without a word, Tristan strides up to Elliana, grasps her arm, and they disappear with a *pop*.

"Oh, shit," Brielle whispers under her breath, and I can't help the laugh that escapes my lips.

"I think your dad's a little pissed," I say, and that is no easy feat. Tristan's usually the calm one, and he wouldn't normally flash with someone without their permission. Then again, he has little patience for anyone who threatens his daughters' safety, including themselves. "Let's walk Dani back."

"It's okay," she says hurriedly. "I can run back."

"It's kind of far, and it's dark. You should know by now that monsters come out at night."

She averts her gaze for a moment. "I, uh, am super-fast. Way beyond normal human fast."

My head tilts as my eyes narrow. "You *are* human, though."

She nods as she wrings her hands in front of her. "It just kind of happened a couple of years ago. I don't know why or how—Papa thinks it was something in the water I drank or even that weird eclipse. But now I can do things like run really fast. You don't need to worry about me."

Ah. So she is one of the norms who's gained special powers and abilities in recent years, like inhuman speed and strength. Our theory so far is that it's an evolution from the magic permeating the air and water around the world because it started happening before that bizarre eclipse she speaks of—the same day the girls had vanished from our world. We've been seeing more and more norms like this, although they're still not common.

Before I can argue with her, Dani hollers a quick goodbye as she takes off toward town, a blur in the night.

"Guess we better get home and save Elli," Brielle says as she spreads her wings.

"We'll flash," I say, hiding my own. "After we find Blossom and Charleigh. And don't think for a minute that you're off the hook with this."

She scowls. "I just thought Elli should have some fun. She's never really met anyone before, and you know that's all she's ever wanted."

"Yeah, well, there's a price for fun."

"And I have to pay it even though it wasn't fun for me?"

Oh, my sweet girl. I almost feel bad for her. Sometimes I wonder if Brie even knows how to have fun. She goes along with Elliana and Charleigh in their escapades, but she's definitely the most responsible of the three. And so far, she's had little interest in boys, too engrossed in how to help civilization return to the way it'd been before she was even born. She never even notices when boys pay her attention, much to Tristan's delight. He fully appreciates being the only man in her life besides her uncles.

He always changes the subject when I bring up Aithan, the man who'd been with Hope in the Space Between—that weird place we may or may not have been taken to after we may or may not have gone to that other, dark world. Those events are all so surreal, and a part of me still wonders if it had been a dream shared with Tristan, Vanessa, and Owen. Probably the part that doesn't want to accept the reality of what we'd been told.

Anyway, Aithan claimed to know the girls in the future—and I believe he deeply cares for them, or at least one. I'm assuming that's Brielle, and I often wonder when and how they'll meet. Will he be her forever person? Her soul mate like Tristan is mine? The Angels never gave us any messages about the girls' mates like they had for Tristan and me, and now I guess they never will, if Heaven's Gates remain sealed. Although I was impressed with the measures Aithan had taken to help my daughters, I still hope that if they really do meet in the future that it's still many years off. Although the twins have technically come of age—whatever that means in this post-Armageddon life—I'm not ready to let my girls go yet.

I heave out my own sigh, understanding Brielle's perspective although she could never understand mine. At least, not until she becomes a mother herself. "We'll talk about it at home," I say.

Tristan works the girls extra hard the next day during training. Or, at least, he attempts to—they're getting better and better at handling whatever he throws at them, whether it's brute strength, magic spells, or other powers. Now he has Charleigh lobbing magic at them, and she's giving them a run for their money.

We're at the beach house in the Florida Keys, a safe place far away from any other living creatures. Our supposed visit to the Space Between had me missing this place terribly, and when we needed a secluded area to train the girls, we often came here with the help of Owen's portals. Of course, with our responsibilities around the world, that isn't as often as I wish it could be.

"The time is coming, Blossom," I say as we watch Charleigh throw a magic spell at Elliana, who easily deflects it and returns one back at the orange-haired witch. My voice is heavy, and my best friend looks over at me, her brow lifted over her big, hazel eyes in question. "We're going to have to tell them the truth. The whole truth. We can't keep it from them any longer. They need to know why this—" I gesture at their training— "and our over-protectiveness is so important."

Blossom nods as she returns her gaze to what we've dubbed the Triple Threat. When they were little, the threat was more of the cuteness variety —they could convince anyone to do anything with a bat of their eyes, especially when they ganged up on a poor unsuspecting soul. Now, the threat is very real. All three are powerful, or at least, the twins will be, when the spell that suppresses their powers is broken and they're fully released. Charleigh's already a force to be reckoned with, nearly as powerful as Owen.

"I can't disagree," Blossom says. "They need to grow into their full potential. I've taken them as far as I can with their mage powers. Owen might be able to take them a little further, but push too much, and they might break the suppression on their own anyway."

It had been Dorian's idea to suppress their powers and alter their memories in the aftermath of that night two years ago. Only minutes after he'd snapped their necks, efficiently ending the destruction they were causing but nearly sending me to the grave myself. He'd known they'd revive because he'd had his own neck snapped a few times—and had also learned it wasn't the first time they'd been . . . "killed."

"Just like vampires," Vanessa had noted when she learned of it—a very different reaction than my own, which was total freak-out, especially when Dorian refused to provide more details. Vanessa's observation made sense since vampire DNA is a part of ours, but Dorian said it's a combination of that along with their Demon and fae DNA, and Tristan and I have discussed whether it has anything to do with them all being marked, as well.

When the twins began to stir after their injuries healed, things got really weird around the abandoned farmhouse we'd taken them to. We'd all been outside, fighting over what we should do next when three birds flew overhead—a rare sight these days—and then dropped from the sky, dead before their bodies thudded to the ground. The trees around the farmhouse began to *melt*, their limbs drooping and dripping and their trunks oozing into puddles in the gray dirt. We all fell silent for a brief moment then flashed inside. Dark energy filled the girls' room before we could even get to it and began to seal the door. One of Dorian's warlocks managed to break through—by casting the magic that suppressed the twins' powers.

The whole situation and how it went down rankled me at first, but I'd known deep within and eventually accepted that suppressing their powers was probably best for everyone. But I'd really hated the idea of altering their memories and fought it vehemently. While the girls were in a magically induced coma, we tried desperately to come up with a better solution.

*"You have no idea what they've been through," Dorian argued after they returned that tragic night in Ravenbury.*

*"And you do?" I demanded. "Have you known where they were all along?"*

*Just like every other time I asked, he didn't answer me directly, but his jaw muscle ticked. "I know enough. I know you don't want your daughters to ever remember the horrors of where they were. And do you really want them to remember what they did to that town?"*

*I scowled. No, I really didn't want them to experience the aftermath of what they'd done—the terror they'd created, the damage to life and property. They would no doubt relive it every time they closed their eyes. They were only sixteen. We'd missed their birthday when they were gone, and this was what they'd come home to? Regret and remorse greater than any fully matured adult could possibly handle?*

*But they needed to know. They needed to understand what they were capable of. They needed to feel that regret and remorse for what they had done. But maybe not yet? Dorian had already ensured they couldn't access their powers anymore. And it wasn't like they'd done any of it on purpose—I was sure of that. Dorian had said they'd been experiencing PTSD, mentally in a different place where they had to fight for survival, and they'd probably suffer with that for a long time, perhaps throughout their lives. Unless we took their memories—at least for a while, until they were mature enough to handle it all better.*

*"There is another option," Dorian offered, and we explored that one—the world on the other side of the gate he'd opened—but it was too risky, putting other realms and worlds in potential danger.*

*"The best solution for now is to keep them close to us and train them ourselves," Tristan said after hashing out other options to come to this only conclusion.*

*Dorian nodded. "They should still have their mage powers, some of their fae abilities, and Amadis power. And their wings, too. That was the deal."*

*My eyes narrowed, still not liking this deal he'd made with the warlock before even discussing it with us. Dorian seemed to be on our side—but was he?*

*"So when they're older and that spell breaks," Tristan continued, "we can give back their memories, too."*

With no other solutions and believing it would probably be best for everyone, I finally agreed to conceal their memories. All of the warnings from Mom and Rina, Bree, the woman Hope in the Space Between had hinted at the need to do everything necessary to protect my daughters until they were older. Burying their memories along with their powers bought us some time to prepare.

I didn't know then that while we were exploring our options, Dorian had already altered everyone else's memories. The people of Ravenbury, including Scout, have a very different recollection of what happened that night. All of the damage had been repaired, the injured healed, and now they vaguely remember something about the girls showing up in their town after being missing for a couple of months. According to them, that same night there'd been some freaky explosion in one of the buildings on the square, caused by a spontaneous combustion. A total coincidence in their minds. And Ranker and his group had been halfway back to Misery's Edge with no memory of seeing me and convinced there was no reason to continue searching for me. He'd dropped the murder charges, never bothering us since.

*"How could you do such a thing?" I demanded the next time I saw Dorian.*

*"I think you're looking for the words, 'thank you.' And you're welcome," he replied cheekily.*

*I stared at my son in disbelief. "You have no right to do that! To interfere in their lives like this!"*

*He shrugged. "They have no idea anything's been done. Their painful memories have been removed. Their lives are no worse off, and your daughters aren't hated and feared. And you don't have to deal with a murder trial."*

*"I could have handled the murder charges. And maybe the girls should be hated and feared."*

*Dorian's brows lowered over his eyes. "Not yet. Their time will come for that, but not yet. Besides, do you think they'd be safe if any of these people remembered what they'd done? They'd be handed over in a heartbeat—to the Ancients or perhaps the Demons, or maybe the dark fae would track them down. Is that what you want?"*

*I growled, hating that I agreed with him—and at the same time feeling a bit of hope. This meant he cared, right? And if he cared in even the least bit, there was still hope for his soul.*

*"If it's so easy for you to take people's memories of that night, why not take everyone's? Why not take ours too?" I asked him.*

*Now his brow lifted as he looked me dead in the eye. "Because you need to remember what your children are capable of."*

Not only could I never forget, but I've had to live with it ever since. Taking the girls' memories has prevented them from having to live with it, too, but the hold wouldn't last much longer. Not when their powers seem to be growing the last few months. All they've known is that they disappeared for a while, and right after we found them, they were cursed and in a coma. When they awoke, they remembered nothing of where they'd been or what happened, just that they had their wings and more powers. We gave them half-truths for their own good and protection.

"We're doing exactly what my mom did to me when I was their age," I say to Blossom.

"Your mom didn't have a choice. That was Amadis protocol, until you went through the *Ang'dora*."

"I still wonder if that's what they did when they were gone . . . that they went through the *Ang'dora*. I can't imagine what that would have been like, all alone."

"I guess we'll know when their memories are returned," she replies. "And at least they had each other."

"I hope. But they still didn't have me to help them through it. And then their powers were taken away right after they'd come into them."

"Everything you've done has been in their best interest, Alexis—just like your mom did for you. You can understand now why she did what she did, why she kept you in the dark and altered your memories. They will understand, too . . . eventually."

She makes a valid point, and I blow out a breath. "I just don't know if they're ready for it all yet."

She looks over at me and tilts her head. "They're not ready or you're not?"

We both know the answer to that, but I'm still stewing over it an hour later when Owen comes through a portal.

"Chandra is ready," he says, leaning over as he braces his hands on his knees. "She's taking us on another field trip."

Blossom claps her hands together and bounces on the balls of her feet. "Yes!"

Chandra has taken the girls to some of the coolest places on Earth—places once overwhelmed with tourists or banned from the public or so obscure that they're nearly impossible to reach without magic. We've visited ancient spiritual sites and ruins, energy vortexes, mineral mines, hot springs, and other wonders scattered around the world. We go partly to see how they've been affected by the war's fallout, partly to educate the girls (and some of us adults) on history, sociology, and anthropology, and always to provide a spiritual connection and a place for meditation and journey. It's been excellent groundwork for the twins to learn how to manage their energy before the full force of their powers return to them, and Tristan and I have enjoyed it, too. But Blossom and Charleigh—and even Owen—really get into it. They say each one has been like a huge energy jolt to their magic.

"Are you okay?" I ask, eyeing Owen as he straightens, his chest lifting and falling rapidly as though he struggles for breath. He looks like he can use such a jolt right about now.

He shakes it off and gives a lopsided grin. "It takes a lot of magic to get where we're going, but it's worth it."

Blossom and Charleigh have to feed him some of their power when he struggles to open a new portal a few minutes later. Once he does and everyone steps through, the girls gasp and Blossom squeals.

I, however, feel like a giant's fist has slammed into my chest.

# CHAPTER 3

*T*he breath whooshes out of me, and my hand flies to my chest, over my heart. My legs feel like noodles, and Tristan grasps my elbow, pulling me into him and holding me up. Electric tingles race through my blood and skin and bones, especially where our bodies connect.

"You okay?" he asks.

Blossom, Chandra, and Owen all turn to stare at me. The girls don't even notice, though, taking in the surroundings. I can't blame them. The vision before us is ... impossible.

"Are we inside a geode?" Charleigh squeals.

"What's wrong?" Blossom asks at the same time.

The sensation is already beginning to fade, and my strength returns. I straighten, and Tristan releases me, but I instantly miss his arms around me. I have a nearly uncontrollable urge to flash away with him to somewhere private. I can't remember the need to be with him being this strong since we were freaking newlyweds or when he first returned from his captivity with the Daemoni.

"I don't know what it is, but I'm fine. I think." I press my hand back to my heart, where the electric tingles have gathered into an unusual energy that feels like . . . *Tristan.* Then I realize it's not my heart the energy swirls around, but the stone embedded in the flesh just above it. "It's the faerie stone."

Chandra's eyes go wide. "Oh! It must be the selenite."

Owen and Blossom turn away again, their gazes sweeping over what appears to be a cave that we've portaled into—a dark cave with an orb of light hanging over our heads in the air, illuminating white crystals that stab out of the walls, the ceiling, and the floor in every direction. Some are larger and longer than Tristan is tall, like fallen crystal trees that stretch almost all the way across the space. Hundreds of much smaller ones cover the ceiling, their points only inches from Tristan's head. It's like a scene from an alien world, but I know we haven't left ours. The beauty that's buried beneath our Earth's crust is astounding.

But the energy buzz … oof, this one is powerful.

Blossom looks at me again, her hand covering her mouth and her already large eyes about to pop out of her head. "Selenite is an energy cleanser," she says. "It purifies the energy of everything around it, including other stones. Chandra, do you think it's affecting her faerie stone?"

The triangular stone, which looks like a ruby or garnet, connects Tristan's emotions to mine and vice and versa, almost like a piece of his heart he's given to me for safe keeping. His mother Bree embedded it in my chest long ago so I couldn't lose it again—in the wrong hands, it could be used as a weapon, since it can effectively control Tristan. I don't know if he still needs that connection between us, which keeps his demonic beast from rising again, after all these years, but it's not something I want to test, either.

"Oh, no. I did not consider that." The dark-eyed woman looks at me with concern etching lines at her mouth, her hands wringing in front of her. I haven't seen her this worried since the war. "Ms. Alexis, I am so very sorry."

I shake my head, then tilt it as I concentrate. "I don't think it's clearing the powers of the stone. If anything, it feels stronger."

"Selenite also charges," Blossom adds, and Chandra's head bobs in a nod as her breath releases in an audible sigh of relief.

"For people, it enhances love and connection, brings joy, and all kinds of other lovely benefits," she says.

"That's exactly what I feel." My arm slips around Tristan's waist, needing his physical touch to help ground the heightened emotions. "Just, like, super strong."

"Whew. Okay. That's not a bad thing. So we can begin." Chandra smiles, then turns and strides over to the girls, who are already exploring.

She begins their lesson about the cave in what had once been Mexico and submerged under water before the war, then goes on to discuss all of those benefits of selenite. She gives all three of them a handmade pendant with a piece of selenite as well as a piece of black tourmaline, also known for clearing negative energies and providing protection. "The wire they're wrapped in is white gold, since I know you two Knight twins are allergic to silver."

I internally cringe at this. "Allergic" is a misnomer, the reason we'd given them when suddenly they couldn't touch or wear silver anymore after they returned. That happens to be a Daemoni and Demon trait, although the twins' reaction isn't nearly as intense. It's another sign, though, of how strong the dark energy is that runs through their blood.

When our lesson is complete, Chandra sits us in a circle for meditation. As my mind quiets, the rest of me picks up even more on the buzz of the mineral. For a while, I feel like I'm floating in front of Heaven's Gates again, trying to connect to the Angels and my ancestors. I can practically *feel* them nearby, but on the other side of the locked gates, which may as well be on the other side of the universe. For all I know, that's exactly where they are—on the far side of the universe. Hell, maybe on the far side of the multiverse, never to be seen again.

Even with this sad thought, I still feel emotionally good when we come out of the meditation. Owen has definitely been recharged by the crystal cave, but before he creates portals to return us home, we flash outside. Blossom takes the girls on a walk to see if they can find any medicinal plants or otherwise useful foliage around while Chandra talks to Tristan and me.

"Their power has certainly grown since I last saw them two months ago," she says. The assessment is why we'd asked for today. She might be a shifter, but she's trained in energy healing, a Reiki master teacher, and all sorts of other magical mystical stuff.

*"Do you know why your grandmother added me to her council?" she asked me one day a few years after the war. She had sensed how hard I'd been fighting to find some kind of balance among all of my responsibilities. As an empath, she felt my emotions and proposed working with me on my chakras and instilling meditation habits.*

*My reply came quickly. "Because you're a good leader."*

She shrugged. "Yes, I am, but so are a lot of shifter alphas. Ms. Katerina came to me because she wanted to ensure she remained open-minded to all possibilities. She didn't want to allow certain religious prescriptions or a single philosophy to color her decisions. She appreciated that I was more spiritually connected than religiously bound and that I could bring a different and broader perspective."

To be honest, this kind of surprised me at the time. I'd always seen Rina as strictly adhering to the Angels' directives.

"As you know, the Angels' messages aren't always clear," Chandra explained. "Rina sometimes had great difficulty interpreting them. But when I brought her a different perspective beyond what she'd learned as a child, brought up in the human-led churches, she was able to make more sense of the messages she was given. She'd learned to connect on a higher level."

"Well, that would be useful," I muttered.

"And that's why I'm here. Use what I bring to your table, Alexis. Let me help in ways others cannot."

So I began working with her on my own spiritual, emotional, and energetical development, and I don't know if I could have survived this long without her. After the whole experience with Hope and the Space Between, Chandra had been the first person I'd gone to for perspective.

"I don't even know if it was real," I said to her as we sat surrounded by crystals in the healing room at her bunker, outside what had been the city of Kolkata. Well, she sat. I'd been pacing while delivering my story. "How can it be?"

"Do you believe all things are possible with Source—with God?" she asked in reply as her dark eyes watched me.

"I do. But other worlds—entire universes? And other devils and gods?" I stopped, tossing my hands in the air before dropping them to my hips. "That Aithan guy is supposedly descended from a god, Chandra. How do I wrap my head around that when I've always been taught and believed in the one God?"

"Step back and think it through, Alexis. If your one God created this amazing, vast universe with everything in it, including the stars and the planets, the galaxies and the black holes, couldn't He have created other universes like it, populated with more of His creations? Could He not have created other beings with power like His and given them dominion over certain worlds or entire universes? Or perhaps these deities, like Christ, are physical versions of Himself or, like Mother Goddess and Gaia, reflections of certain aspects of Himself—archetypes or avatars. Think of it this way—they said Aithan's ancestor Aion is the god of all time, yes?" I nodded. "So could Aion not be a physical version of God who is responsible for that one aspect of the universe—the conjunction of time and space? Could Aphrodite not be the feminine energy of the Divine, responsible for love and fertility?"

I stared at the ground, my brow furrowing as I thought this through—it was something my brain could wrap around a little easier now. "Okay, but that world we went to, on the other side of the gate Dorian opened, was so much like ours. Not a new creation but a literal copy of how our world had been before the war—except there's no Amadis and Daemoni and other small differences, like more types of supernatural races."

"So not an exact copy," she corrected. "Perhaps the All-Powerful fractured time and space and sent duplicates of a world or even a whole universe into alternate dimensions and realms. Does it not make sense that someone with powers and creativity like His might be curious to see how differently His creations would evolve over time with just the slightest changes? He could have put some types of creations in one world, universe, or realm, and different types in others."

The conversation made my head spin with the possibilities. But in the end, I finally came to think that just maybe the experience with Hope and Aithan had been real.

"So I guess you think there's truth in what they said about the dark worlds and the Thrones, too?" I asked her.

She tugged on her long black braid, pulling it through her hands as she considered this. "Anything is possible, so yes. We know He created both light and dark. One cannot exist without the other—and they must be in balance. It's not only feasible that these dark worlds exist, but that Source created them equally and populated the dark worlds just as He did the light ones. Does that mean He created evil? I can't pretend to know that was His intention. I do know that dark does not have to mean evil, though. It's still just energy. Whether it's harmful or helpful is all in how we manage that energy, what we do with it. And if His other creations are anything like the ones on this world, then there can be those who don't manage their energy well, regardless of how dark or light it is. Those who decide they want more power, more control—that one world is not enough for them. That balance is not enough. When they've gone that far, they will likely stop at nothing to have it all."

. . .

And that was exactly what I feared—that having it all meant having my daughters.

We've had many discussions about it since then, including her belief that the place most people call Hell doesn't exist, even though I've been there. She suggests that had been another one of these dark worlds, overtaken by a Throne—Satan, in this case. Her perspective of Hell is more aligned with Hope's, more of a broader concept that encompasses these dark worlds and their inhabitants, but not as a place created to imprison sinful souls. She can't believe that a benevolent, loving God would create such a place—or that He would want these souls He created to harbor such fear that they would be afraid to truly live and experience the beautiful world He gave them.

"God is love, and fear is the opposite of love, yes? How can God be love if He wants to evoke fear in His name in even the youngest of children?" she'd asked me one time, and truthfully, I didn't have a confident answer.

But I fully understand why Rina brought Chandra onto her council—and why she will forever be a part of mine. She's become more than an advisor, though. She's a mentor and a teacher, not only for the girls, but for the rest of us as well.

Because Chandra detects energy better than some mages and she doesn't see the twins every day, unlike Blossom and Owen, she can take a better measure of how much they've changed.

"I agree it won't be long before they break the curse on their own," she says. "The pendants and other tools I've given them over the years can help, and we've all trained them as best as we can to this point. The rest is up to them."

I blow out a heavy breath and nod. Isn't that what Blossom and I had just been talking about earlier today? "Thank you for all of your help with this, Chandra. You've brought a layer of expertise we didn't really have. Blossom's good at it, but not quite at your level. Plus, I think it's been good for the girls to have someone with a little more distance to teach them this."

She smiles. "Yes, I think it's a little easier for the students if they're not too emotionally bound to their teacher."

"Oh, they do adore you," I say quickly. "As do I."

"Oh, yes, I know." She pats my hand. "But it is not the same as what they feel for Blossom. It is a good thing, Alexis. We have done good here. I am glad I could help."

Owen creates a portal to take Chandra home, and we've barely said goodbye as the portal closes behind her when one of the girls shouts something unintelligible from around the side of the hill, followed by a high-pitched voice we don't know. I sense the strange presence, and Tristan and I barely glance at each other before flashing to them, Owen popping in right after us.

Blossom and the three girls are in formation and dropped into fighting stance, facing two creatures that make my jaw drop. With heads and upper torsos of a woman but lower bodies and legs of a spider, they look like something that crawled out of Hell itself. Notching their bows with arrows, they scream again and skitter toward Elliana, and then I notice another, different kind of creature that looks like an alien dragonfly buzzing through the air toward Brielle.

Before anyone else can act, Charleigh slashes her hands in the air, and the dragonfly bounces off an invisible shield before it reaches my daughter. The young mage quickly follows with another spell, blasting the thing several feet back, where it drops to the dirt, perfectly still. Brielle directs a nearby brittlebush's roots to grow upward from the ground and slither around one of the spider's bodies, climbing up its torso and squeezing the air out of it, while Elliana shoots a spear of flame at the other spider and Charleigh hits it with her own spell. They both fall to the ground dead, their legs curling inward.

It all happens in a second before it's over, and I'm left there gaping at the girls.

"What did I tell you?" Owen says quietly at my side. "She's your girl. She acted faster than any of us, and Brielle's possibly still alive because of it."

Tristan crosses the brush to the first assailant's side, but then several more she-spiders spring up out of nowhere.

"Owen, get the girls home!" Tristan bellows as he puts himself between the creatures and the rest of us.

"I'll shield him," Charleigh yells at Owen, already throwing the spell out to surround Tristan.

Owen begins opening the portal next to me while the girls and Blossom start lobbing spells as Tristan's backup. The spiders close in, moving strangely, otherworldly, and I have a moment to realize they crawl on nine legs, rather than the expected eight. I shoot a blast of electricity at one approaching from the side, the current slowing it, at least.

"Come on, Alexis, you first," Owen says as he stretches the portal wider.

"Not a chance. Brielle and Elliana! Charleigh and Blossom! Get out of here!"

As a group, they move closer, still casting spells as they go, blocking the flying arrows. I cover them when they get closer.

"Go, Elli & Brie!" Charleigh orders them when they hesitate. Blossom practically pushes them through. "You, too, Mom."

"I'm not leaving you here," Blossom protests.

"She's right behind you," I say, motioning Blossom to hurry. As soon as she's through, I move to Charleigh's side. "Go. We got this."

"That's my shield on Uncle Tristan," she argues.

"He'll be fine. Just go!"

She backs up toward the portal and finally ducks through it. It's like the spider-things know we're not protected anymore, because they charge at the three of us.

"Your turn, Alexis," Owen hollers while Tristan holds his ground, shooting fire and using his own power to block their arrows. Finally, he sweeps his hand in an arc from left to right, and they all freeze, totally motionless.

I can't argue with Owen any longer, so I duck through the portal, hoping they're right behind me. I come out in the woods by The Loft, but the portal closes up as soon as I'm through it.

"What the hell, Owen?" I shout, although the warlock wouldn't have heard me.

"What happened?" Brielle asks from behind me. "Why didn't they come?"

"I don't know." My hands drop to my hips as I stare at the air where the portal should have been. Another minute or two passes by with no new portal, no Owen or Tristan. "I'll just have to flash back to them. Make sure they're okay."

"I'm sure they are," Blossom says. "It's Tristan and Owen, for Angels' sake. They can take care of themselves."

I nod. I know she's right. But those … *things*. I don't know what they are. They don't seem to be of this world. What if they're from the dark one? What if the gate has opened again?

"They might need my Amadis power, though," I say, grasping at straws because I just need to know for sure that they're okay now that I know my girls are safe.

"After all this time, you still doubt?" Owen teases from off to our right. He and Tristan jog down the slope of the hill where their new portal had dropped them. "We had to take a detour to make sure those things didn't follow us back here."

Tristan's gaze travels over the girls and then to me before he grins, seeing we're okay.

"That was fun," he says. He rubs his hand over Charleigh's head, ruffling her hair. "Good job, Mini Char. I think you might have a future here."

Smoothing her hand over her orange locks, Charleigh beams up at him and then her mom before those orangish-brown eyes swing over at me with expectation.

I lift my hands in surrender. "You definitely proved yourself. But I need to discuss it with your parents."

"I'm over eighteen," she reminds me. As if I need to be reminded. None of them ever let us forget. Not that there's really a legal age anymore, but it's how we've brought them all up—eighteen still equals adulthood, as far as we're concerned, because there has to be some kind of line. Right?

"Humor me," I say with a grin.

I can tell she tries to suppress an eye-roll as she turns back to Elliana and Brielle, and the three of them begin the trek back to The Loft. Blossom and I walk alongside each other behind them.

"Are you ready for this, mama?" I ask her.

"Not really," she says on an exaggerated sigh, but then she bumps her shoulder into mine. "It's a true honor, though, Alexis. And Charleigh is something else. I think one day soon she may even give Owen a run for his money. I will never stop worrying about her, but I know it's what she wants. What she's always wanted."

So two days later, we gather the people of The Loft outside for a formal ceremony to swear Charleigh in as my daughters' sworn protector. She's now officially their Owen.

And an hour after that, the three of them are planning a trip to

Ravenbury.

"I'm sorry, but what?" I ask when Elliana comes into my office to tell me they're leaving.

"We're going to Ravenbury," she says slowly, as if I'm a child. "Brielle wants to check on the generator since she hasn't been back since getting it online again. And we have some healing salves to take to them."

"Who's 'we'?" I ask, already surmising.

"Brielle, Charleigh, and me. And Sasha, of course," she adds quickly.

"I think the proper way to approach this is to say, 'Mom, we would like to go to Ravenbury, so we can help them with X. When can we go?'"

She rolls her eyes. "We don't technically need your permission. We are adults. And we're just doing our jobs—the jobs *you* assigned us."

Suppressing a growl, I stand from behind my desk and lean my hands on the top. "Okay, then, if you want to be treated like adults and members of my guard, act like it. In that case, the proper way to approach this is to say, "Boss, Matriarch, my *Queen*, Ravenbury is in need of our services. We would like to volunteer to be on the team.'"

"Mom," she whines.

"Elliana," I respond, and we stare at each other for a moment. "Look. I know you think you're all grown up and that somehow makes you invincible, but just the other day, we were attacked by unknown entities. That could happen again."

"We were in a place nobody had been for over two decades, with strangely mutated creatures. We know the dangers around here. Besides, we can flash to Ravenbury and back. No wilderness. No hikes. There and back."

We've had a few theories of what those hybrid creatures had been in Mexico, one of the less sinister being that they're simply new mutations from the black magic. Of course, that's one of the new priorities issued to some of my people, led by Tristan—to figure out exactly what the hell they are and why they attacked. Because there are all kinds of theories and implications of it.

"There and back, huh?" I ask Elliana, lifting a brow. As if I don't know the real reason she's so anxious to go.

She lifts a shoulder. "Well, I mean, we'll help wherever they need us while we're there, so it might be a little longer. No reason to waste a trip."

"And?"

"You're going to make me say it?"

"Why don't you want to?"

She scowls, then blows out a breath. "Okay, fine, yes, I want to see Dani again. She's ... I like her, Mom."

"Now, that wasn't so hard, was it? And I'm fully aware just how much you like her. I saw it with my own eyes the other night." She averts her gaze, sucking in the side of her bottom lip, and I can tell she's gnawing on the inside of it. "Elli, you know we weren't mad because you were making out with someone, right?" She doesn't answer, only shrugs. "We were worried because we couldn't find you. You and Brielle aren't like other people. Your dad and I have enemies—all of our people do—and we know from experience that they like to go after our children."

She sighs and looks back up at me. "Yes, we know Dorian's story. But we're not eight, Mom, and you know we aren't defenseless. You have to let us go at some point."

I internally cringe at her words. "It's not just about your age. How would you feel if I disappeared without telling anyone where I was going, and you couldn't find me anywhere, knowing there are creatures out there who'd like me dead? It's simply common courtesy, so people know not to worry. All you have to do is tell someone—anyone—where you will be, so we at least know where to start looking if you don't come back."

"Okay. I get it. I'm sorry."

I'm not so sure she does. In fact, I'm pretty sure she doesn't, and she won't until she herself is put in that situation. "So do you want to try your approach again?"

She glowers. "No. It's probably too late now anyway."

She stomps out of my office and across the conference room. I see Charleigh and Brielle waiting for her out in the tunnel. Tristan stops to say something to them before coming inside, Brielle right behind him.

"Mom, we are overdue to check on Ravenbury's power generator, and I fear if they have problems, they won't know how to fix it. I've assembled a team, and we can leave right away with your permission."

I can't help the chuckle. Elli's apparently too proud to admit she was wrong, but not to send her sister in to do it right. "And who is this team?"

"Myself, Elliana, our sworn protector Charleigh, and Sasha, another loyal protector. We will flash there, do our work, and flash home, no detours. We are well protected, including with our own training. Please give us the chance to prove to you that we can handle missions on our own."

I glance at Tristan, who's smiling behind her, a glint in his eye. He gives a quick nod.

"You have three hours. I expect you back at home base before dark."

She salutes while smiling at the same time. "Yes, ma'am."

"And so it begins," I murmur as she hurries out of the conference room to deliver the news. I look up at Tristan, who still stands on the other side of my desk. "Did you have a hand in that?"

"I only advised they approach you the way they want to be treated."

Well, I can't argue with that. That's exactly what I had requested of Elliana. "This is just the beginning, you know. Our girls are growing up." I drop into my seat, my heart already hurting. I still see them as my little babies. "Way too fast, at that."

"Let them prove themselves, as Brielle said." He sits and stretches his arms across the desk to take my hands. "And then, Lex, you know what we need to do."

I sigh. "Yes, I know. We'll need to plan for it first. I want to do it in a controlled environment. I imagine they'll be extremely pissed at us, and we'll have little chance against their full powers."

One corner of his mouth lifts. "We'll let them simmer down first. And it will definitely be done in a controlled environment."

We discuss where that should be, debating if the beach house would be isolated enough or if we should take them to Amadis Island for this. I say we don't need to decide quite yet, and then keep putting it off. I'm not ready. I'm worried about them. I'm worried about their reaction. I'm worried the other factions will find out. I'm worried about all of the potential consequences, whether they're real or not.

To be honest, I'm fucking scared. For them. For all of us.

In the meantime, the girls return to Ravenbury almost every day for the next week, for one reason or another. Elliana comes home each time in the best mood I've seen her in since ... well, since forever. And that's another reason I can't bring myself to make solid plans for disclosing everything to them—I don't want to ruin this time for her. And what we have to tell her will definitely ruin it.

Then one day I go to Ravenbury with them, only for us to be greeted with devastating news.

"I'm sorry, Elliana," Scout says, "but Dani and Miguel left last night. He found out his friend is living in Misery's Edge."

I can literally feel my daughter's heart break as though it's my own.

# CHAPTER 4

"*I* think it's a good thing she doesn't have her full powers yet," Blossom whispers two days later as we watch Elliana in the sparring ring with Tristan. He's the only one who can—and will gladly—take the pummeling she's given to anyone who dares to get in the ring with her. Vanessa probably would, but she and Owen are on a mission to see if they can find out what those things were that attacked us in Mexico. Of course, I could probably handle her, too, but we aren't about to take any chances. Not because I'm the Amadis matriarch but because a young woman and her mother probably shouldn't have that kind of violent energy exchange, especially with how heightened her emotions are already. And especially because I won't let her run off to Misery's Edge to chase after some girl who apparently couldn't even write a note to say goodbye. Apparently, I'm the worst mother and leader to ever exist because of that, according to Elli anyway.

"No kidding," I agree with my best friend. "We probably wouldn't have a Loft anymore. Actually, I'm kind of surprised we still do, as it is."

A crowd has gathered in the training area of The Loft to watch the spectacle of two super-powers sparring. Elliana seems to be eating up the attention, putting on quite the show of her control over the elements. While she displays her power with an air of cockiness, though, I sense what nobody else can, except maybe Brielle—the grief and pain and despair she's trying to bury. My heart hurts along with hers, but I can feel that dark energy growing within her, and I can't deny that it scares me.

"On the other hand," Sheree says from my other side, "maybe turning her focus on the truth and mastering her full powers is the distraction she needs."

I look over at her, and she returns my gaze with raised brows. She makes a good point, and when I discuss it that night with Tristan, he agrees.

"It's time," he says as he stretches out on the bed. "I worry what will happen if we wait any longer."

"We all do." I exhale a heavy breath before snuggling into his side. "Tomorrow then. We'll go to the beach house, just the four of us and Owen and Vanessa to stand guard."

His arms wrap around me, pulling me closer. "Sounds like a plan."

As my mom used to say, "Man plans, God laughs." Or the Angels do —or Demons or whoever. I don't even know anymore. After a night of tossing and turning, I walk into the girls' room early the next morning to wake them up, but not only are they already awake, but they appear to be in a standoff. While they might be silent, I'm certain words are being exchanged with that twin telepathy thing they have with each other—and by the looks on their faces, I'm sure many of those words are expletives. Brielle stands in her nightclothes by her bed, arms crossed over her chest and giving her sister a death glare. Elliana's dressed in fighting leathers, her backpack on her bed and curiously full of clothes and weapons, from what I can see. Her gaze is locked with Brielle's, looking just as dangerous.

"What's going on?" I ask, my brows pinching together. When neither answer, I try to check their minds, but their shields are up and strong. "Elliana?" She doesn't acknowledge me, doesn't break the lock she and Brielle hold on each other. "Brielle?"

Brie flinches, scowls, and without looking at me, says, "Elli's leaving for Misery's Edge."

"I'm sorry, what?" I ask, but it's drowned out by my other daughter.

"Brielle!" Elliana shouts. "How could you?"

"If the roles were reversed—if it were me chasing after a boy—what would you say, Elli?" Brielle demanded.

Her gaze averting, finally breaking her hold on her twin, Elliana frowns and huffs out a breath. But then she looks up with renewed gusto. "It's not just about a girl, though. It's about *my* life. *My* freedom."

"I'm sorry, what?" I ask again.

Elliana finally looks at me. "I'm done here, Mom. I will never find what I need to be happy here. I've proven that I can protect myself, yet you won't let me on your demon assassination team. So what am I supposed to do? Just keep training day after endless day for no fucking reason?"

"Elli—"

"I'm over eighteen," she interrupts, her voice rising—along with the energy swirling around her. "You can't stop me. It's time I go live *my* life!"

I lift my hands, fingers spread, not quite in surrender but in a soothing gesture. "Just hold on a minute. Let's talk about this. We have a lot to talk about, actually."

She shakes her head. "I don't want to hear it anymore. I know why you're so protective of us. We were kidnapped or whatever just like Dorian, and yeah, we were cursed, which fucking sucks. But we're not *him*, Mom. We're not Dorian! We are our own people and just because he left you doesn't mean we will. But you know what? If you don't back the hell off and let us live our lives, we just might. Sometimes, I can't blame him. Sometimes, I'm tempted to go live with the Daemoni, too, just to get away from *you*!"

I feel like I've been slapped, visibly flinching as my breath catches.

"Elli," I whisper.

"You can't keep us forever, Mother. You *have* to let us go!"

Her words echo some of the last I heard from Dorian when he was still *my* Dorian. If she only knew how much she is like him. Tears prick the backs of my eyes—tears of both rage and sorrow—but the weight of a large, comforting hand on the small of my back calms me.

"That's enough, Elliana," Tristan says, his voice deep and calm but commanding, and when she opens her mouth to argue with him, too, he gives her a withering look that would make the toughest of men bow to their knees. *I dare you*, his eyes say, and she doesn't dare. "We're going to the beach house, including you, and not just for another day of endless training. We need to talk to you both. And if you still feel the need to run off and join the circus, at least you'll be armed with information you're lacking now."

Her eyes flash, and I wonder if she decides to argue with him after all, but then her brows lower. "What kind of information? And what's a circus?"

Two hours later, while Vanessa and Owen scope out the surrounding area, the four of us are on the lawn of the beach house, going through our Aikido forms. Not training, Tristan insisted when Elliana balked, but going through the routine movements that would allow us all to calm down and come to center. It's the next best thing to having Chandra here. But not exactly the same. I can't quiet my mind, and Chandra herself probably wouldn't even be able to help with that, if I'm being honest. Not as I mentally prepare for the speech I'm about to give my daughters—the truth of what happened and what they'd done, what we've done in response, and what's still to come. How do you tell your children that you've been lying to them for years?

My mother and grandmother would know. Secrets were the Amadis way, after all, at least when it came to the daughters before they went through the *Ang'dora*. I ache for their presence now, but know I no longer have their support. Chandra says I was blessed to be able to see my ancestors in the flesh after they'd transitioned to the Otherworld, but just because I can't see them physically anymore doesn't mean they're not still with me.

"I've never seen my own ancestors," she'd said during an energy healing session, "but I know they are here with me, all the time, along with my spirit guides. I *feel* them."

She'd known by then what had happened when we'd been on the cliff on Amadis Island right before the weird eclipse—about my visit to Heaven's Gates when they slammed shut—but I don't think she fully understood. I can't ever feel them, no matter how hard I've tried. Sometimes, especially while in the Memorial Garden, I can feel Char's presence or even Solomon's. I can almost hear them speaking to me. But not Mom's and Rina's. I may not be completely alone, but it's them I need right now. And they're just ... gone. Completely and utterly gone.

"Alexis?" Tristan says. My eyes fly open, and my mind snaps back to the task in front of me. We're all sitting cross-legged on the ground near the beach, after finishing a final breathing exercise. He looks at me expectantly, before silently inquiring, "*You're sure you want to do this? I can—*"

I give a slight shake of my head. "*No, it needs to be me.*"

"*You're not alone in this. How about we do it together? After all, we both made the decision.*" He holds his hand out to me, and I take it, scooting over to sit closer to him in front of our daughters.

"Okay," I start, heaving out one more exhale. "We have some things to tell you that might be … difficult … to both say and hear, but it's important for you to know. You're old enough now to understand and shoulder the weight of what it all means."

"You gave us the sex talk eons ago, Mom," Brielle quips, and Tristan cringes.

"Trust me—I remember," I reply drily. Blossom and I had done that rite of passage together with all three girls several years ago, and the entire Loft will never forget that day, especially with Elli's very loud reaction and how the other two loved to publicly tease her about it every chance they had for the following week. "Unfortunately, this isn't quite so … fun." I pause for another breath to focus. "Okay, so … I don't know if you girls remember, but when you were very young, just six years old, you did something that nobody else ever has been able to do."

"We opened a portal," Elliana says impatiently. "We know. And Owen does it all the time."

"It wasn't an ordinary portal, though," Tristan says. "It wasn't a portal at all, but a gate—to another world in another dimension. A gate that should have never been opened, to a world we should never know about."

The girls exchange a look, and when they're silent for a drawn-out moment, I know they're doing that twin mind-reading thing again.

"It's an evil world, isn't it?" Brielle asks, her voice small as her brown-eyed gaze sweeps up to us, and my heart clenches. "I remember …"

"What do you remember?" I demand, almost too sharply. Has the spell already been broken? Do they remember those events of two years ago? Do they remember where they'd gone—and what happened when they returned?

"I remember you and Dad being mad and almost … scared. Worried. We were so proud of ourselves because we opened a portal for our friends, but you yelled at Owen to close it and make it go away."

I quietly released the breath I'd been holding. She only remembers the incident of when they were six, not the tragedies of when they were sixteen.

"But you're saying that wasn't an ordinary portal? That it goes to another world—an evil one in another dimension?" Elli asks, her eyes narrowing. "How is that even possible? Like other worlds and dimensions?"

I shrug and feel like I'm channeling both Sheree and Chandra when I say, "With our Creator, anything is possible, is it not?"

"So why did we open it?" Brielle asks. "*How?*"

"You two have unusual powers," I start. "Powers like nobody in this world, except maybe your brother. And they're stronger than anything anyone in this world has ever experienced—except, again, maybe your brother. We don't know yet. We won't un—"

"Unless the curse on us is ever broken," Brielle interrupts. "The curse from the Daemoni warlock that's suppressing our powers, that put us into the coma."

"Well—" I pause again. Now we're getting into the hard part, and I need a moment to brace myself.

"Wait," Elli says in that moment between breaths. "Are you saying our powers are what opened that gate?"

"Yes," Tristan answers. "You two and Dorian are uniquely able to do that."

"And it goes to an evil world because *we're* evil," Brielle concludes.

My heart tightens, and I lean over and grasp her hand, giving it a squeeze. "Oh no, honey. Not at all. Don't think that for one minute."

"But we feel it—that same darkness. I remember it. We still feel it. If you think we don't, you've been fooling yourselves." She glances over at her twin, who looks away, lifting her shoulder in a small shrug.

I shake my head. "You've told me about it, in your own ways. So yes, I know there's a darkness in you, but you know what? There is in me, too. You know who my sperm donor was. And you know your dad's history. Aunt Vanessa's ... Uncle Owen's ... Everyone has some darkness to them, even Aunt Sheree."

"But not like us," Elli says flatly.

Unable to deny that theirs is different, I sigh. This conversation isn't exactly going how Tristan and I had planned.

Tristan speaks up. "That's not the point. The point is that we're all aware of it. And we need to be diligent about keeping it under control. That's why—"

"That's why you're not even trying to break the curse on us," Elli interrupts, misunderstanding.

"That's why we train you so hard," Tristan corrects with much more patience than I'm able to hold onto. I'm on the verge of just blurting everything out before they can interrupt or reroute us again, to hell with the strategy and planned words to make it as easy for them to accept as possible. Now that we've started, I just want it to be over with. "We want to make sure you are masters of control, of yourselves."

"Maybe you shouldn't try to break the curse," Brielle suggests. "That's not a bad idea, if you think we're going to be so awful."

"You're not going to be awful," I growl, adamant that they understand this. That they have a choice. They will *always* have a choice. "And breaking the—"

Elli interrupts once again. "Oh, my angels! That's why you're so overbearing, isn't it? Because you think we really are going to go all Dorian on you!"

My fear of their reaction suddenly dissipates with her hurtful words, and my patience snaps, the words falling out of my mouth before I can stop them. We'll just have to deal with the consequences of our actions and hope they don't go "all Dorian" on anybody else.

"You know what? Yes, we're worried about you. If you think you've felt the darkness already, you don't have any idea what you're in for because that's suppressed, too. It will *feed* your powers, and we need to make sure you're mature enough and strong enough to handle it because not even your father and I are able to stop you."

"How do you know?" Brielle asks.

I lean closer, up on my knees to give me some height, some leverage, and continue without answering her. "And I'm so overbearing, as you say, Elliana, so *protective* because you're in more danger than we've ever told you about before, and not just you. When all of the other factions know what you have done with that gate—when they learn what else you are capable of once the spell is broken—when the Daemoni, the Demons, even the fae all know, they *will* come after you, either to capture and use you for your powers or to kill you because of them. So you're damn right that I want to be sure you absolutely can protect yourselves *and* everyone around you before we unleash your full potential. Your lives are at stake— and so is the rest of the world's."

I give them a moment to process that before continuing, leaning back on my heels as they stare at me.

Then Brie asks again, "But how do you *know*?"

Ugh! This is not at all how we were supposed to lead them to the truth. So many secrets to reveal, and none of it's coming out right. My mind churns through everything there's still left to say—things we think should come from us before they remember the actual events so they can be more prepared for the emotional onslaught that will surely follow, as well as the whole bit about them being Throne-marked. But I'm still not sure what that even means. Unfortunately, when we break the spell on them, we're probably going to find out.

Maybe even sooner.

As I'm still gathering my thoughts, Owen's voice jumps into my mind. *"Boss lady, we have a problem."*

He doesn't even finish the thought when Tristan and I both sense the presence at the same time, our wings exploding from our backs.

# CHAPTER 5

*T*ristan springs into the air without a word, leaving me to give a quick order to the girls to stay put—no matter what—and wait the two seconds for Vanessa to arrive to ensure they do just that. Then I launch into the sky and fly to the east, following Tristan. I catch up in time to see two male forms in the air, the winged one dressed in leather launching himself at the wingless one wearing a suit. Dorian blasts his power at Tristan, who tumbles backward in the sky before righting himself and shooting a burst of fire from his palm.

"Tristan!" I shout with disbelief.

Dorian easily deflects and is about to retaliate when I fly in between them.

"What the hell?" I growl as I hold my arms up between them—as if I can stop them if they really want to hurt each other.

"You brought them here?" Tristan barks, flicking his hand toward the east—toward a large group of Daemoni moving on the ground. We haven't seen that much activity in one place from the Daemoni since before the war.

"I diverted them," Dorian seethes through a clenched jaw. "And I'm here to warn you."

I spin to face him. "Of what?"

"The time has come. I don't know how much longer I can keep our secret. Victor's down there, trying to take my place as leader of the Daemoni. And that won't be good for any of us."

I peer down at the group of about eighty or so who are miles away, heading back east toward Miami, away from the beach house—they'd come way too close for comfort, though. Of course Victor would go there if he wanted to find us. Vanessa's twin and my half-brother knows about the beach house, knows it's a place we've used in the past as a personal safe house.

"Why are they suddenly so interested?" I ask Dorian.

"Everyone knows now. The Ancients, the Demons, Victor. The fae, too."

"About the twins?"

"About everything—the twins, their powers, the gate they opened, what that means. The fae have figured it out, and they're on their way—the dark *and* the light."

"The dark fae?" Tristan demands, his voice rough, only slightly calmer than a minute ago. "That's what attacked us last week, isn't it—the dark fae?"

His question seems rhetorical, but Dorian nods. "Their beasts, yes. Whatever's behind that gate my sisters opened—it's affected the faerie realm, too. The fae courts have been searching for the cause of it ever since the twins opened it the first time."

"Twelve years ago?" I ask. When he nods again, I momentarily wonder what took them so long, then I remember how time moves differently there.

"And now they've figured it out. Or, at least, they're close enough to the truth to know the twins are a part of it all. The dark fae haven't been in this realm in thousands of years, but now they're coming. The light fae, too. The Demons know, as well, either from the fae or some other source. There's a major demon, Shamara, who's on the prowl, wanting the twins. The Ancients have had their attention on her for other reasons, and I've kept the Daemoni focused on hunting her down, but she's powerful and she's sneaky as fuck. Unfortunately, we've lost track of her. With all the other factions on the move—we're out of time and I'm out of excuses. If any of them discover how I've played them, they'll find a way to kill me, and then you'll have more problems on your hands."

My gaze swings between Tristan and Dorian, all of us hovering a hundred feet over the ground. "We were just about to tell them everything. Then we were going to break the spell."

Dorian's mouth turns down. "That will only attract more attention to them."

"They're going to blast right through the spell on their own anyway. Their powers are growing exponentially," Tristan says, which makes Dorian scowl harder.

"At least they'll be able to protect themselves," I add. "What do *you* think we should do?"

"There's still the one option," Dorian hedges, one brow lifting, and I open my mouth, but he holds a hand up, stopping me. "Reconsider, Mom. They'll be safe in that other world. They can hide there while we address everything here."

I shake my head. I can't stand the thought, even while a small part of me admits he might be right.

Tristan and I had checked out that other world, the one Dorian had opened a gate to not long after the twins had opened theirs the first time. He'd closed his and cloaked it right away—I don't even know if the Ancients ever learned what he'd done. While the girls were in their coma after...that awful night...Dorian took us to the gate, proposing our other option at the time: we could hide the twins in this other world. It wasn't a real solution, though—taking our girls to another place with their powers and nobody truly on their side to help them would have been disastrous for all the worlds.

The visit had been heartbreaking for me. I'd felt a homesickness for a place—and time—we could never return to in our own world. I would have loved for our girls to be able to live there and experience life more like the one I'd grown up in. But Tristan and I wouldn't have been able to stay. We have responsibilities here. And there was no way I could leave the twins there, not when they were so young, and especially if they were as dangerous as we'd been warned. As we'd witnessed ourselves. They'd needed us then.

But things are different now.

"You're going to have to decide soon," Dorian continues when I don't reply. "Another war is coming. I can't stop it anymore, and neither can you. You need to decide where you want your daughters while everyone fights over them."

He looks over in the direction of the Daemoni, and when I follow his gaze, I see they've stopped their trek to the east, and some are starting to turn back around. Then they suddenly all start running to the west, toward the beach house, vampires blurring and shifters phasing on the fly.

"Fuck," Dorian mutters right before he disappears in a dark streak across the sky.

"Tristan!" I gasp as the Daemoni close in on the beach house, but my husband is also already gone.

I flash to the house in time to see Owen whisking the girls and Sasha through a portal then practically shoves Vanessa through, insisting she stay with the twins. Daemoni soar toward him and the passage. Owen shoots a spell at a couple of mages who appear to be trying to keep the portal open. Tristan blasts his power, knocking a pack of wolves racing for the magical opening to the ground in lifeless heaps. I happen to appear right in Victor's path, and I charge at him, flying up and stopping above him, grabbing his head and twisting until I hear the snap and his body falls to the ground. It won't kill him, but it takes him out long enough. At the same time, the portal closes and disappears, leaving Tristan, Owen, and me as more Daemoni in all shapes and forms charge at us.

And then they stop.

Dorian drops in front of them, and several growl and snarl, but don't attack. Others gaze at him in surprise, and my own jaw hangs in disbelief as my stomach rolls.

For in each of his hands, he grips a fistful of hair—hair still attached to heads that are not at all attached to bodies.

Blood drips from shredded skin where the throats should have been. A pair of dead eyes stare back at me as Dorian lifts the heads into the air.

"I warned you not to disobey me!" my son bellows, and the entire throng of Daemoni shrink back. "An army that can't follow orders is an army that falls to its enemies."

He continues yelling at his people as Tristan's hand wraps around my shoulder and pulls me back, but my legs don't move, as though my feet are welded to the ground. I can't believe what I'm seeing, even after all the stories I'd heard. Even after his warning to let him go because he's a monster. Yet, I'm not about to leave my son now. Not with a hundred or more Daemoni who can't decide if they want to obey him—or kill him.

"*Get out of here, Mom*," Dorian growls in my mind. "*Whatever happens next, you don't want to see.*"

When Tristan's arm snakes around my waist, I lean into him. Taking the chance while we have it, we flash away with Owen following our trail, to a safe spot where he opens a new portal to home.

Tristan tries to calm me once we're safely on the other side, but his efforts are futile. Too much just happened, not the least of which being that Dorian killed two of his own. The repercussions of that, especially while protecting us, the enemy, would surely be deadly. I attempt to console myself that he's supposedly died before, but all I can think is if anyone could figure out how to kill him for good, it's the Ancients. And when they find out what he just did—

"We shouldn't have left him," I scream in frustration. "We need to go back and help him!"

"Give him some credit, Lex," Tristan replies, grabbing my hand and pulling me to him, forcing me to focus on his face, on his words. "He knows what he's doing with them. He always has, hasn't he?"

"Except he'd just been saying that he'd toed the line for too long. Well, now he just blatantly crossed it."

"The girls were already safe, and we could have escaped without his help. He knows that."

I tilt my head forward to lean against his chest. "You think he had a plan?"

He doesn't answer for a moment before he releases a sigh. "I sure fucking hope so."

"*You cannot be here!*" The deep voice booms in my mind, making me jump.

Whipping around, I find a large creature with a head the size of a car, a body the size of a bus, and teal and blue scales clamoring up the hill that slopes down in front of us. I notice our surroundings for the first time, the familiar lake we use as our water source—and share with the dragons —off to my left.

"What the hell, Owen?" I ask, turning on him, where he and Vanessa stand between the dragon and the girls. "Why'd you bring us *here?*"

"I didn't want to get too close to The Loft in case any of the Daemoni tried to follow," he says.

The dragon shrinks down to human size, then morphs into his human shape—Ethan-shape to be exact, in all his naked gloriousness. And I hate to say it, considering I have my own perfect man, but Ethan's body is definitely glorious. But he's boiling mad, which seems to be his go-to emotion, at least when it comes to us. Smoke escapes his nostrils as he fumes at Owen's answer.

"You thought you could bring Daemoni *here*?" he growls, and I realize just how close we are to his nest.

"I figured you can handle them. A little barbecue for the clan would be fun, wouldn't it? I hear they taste good with ketchup." Owen grins.

Ethan's dark brows furrow together over his royal blue eyes. Of course he doesn't get the joke—he'd been held captive in Hell for centuries before the war and has no understanding of pop culture of the Before time. Dismissing Owen, he turns to us. "You need to leave. Now. We will offer you no refuge."

I lift my hands in surrender. "No worries. We don't need refuge."

"Are you sure about that? Have you been back to your lair?"

I internally snicker at his term for The Loft. The first time he'd called it that, years ago, I'd teased Tristan for days about how we all lived at my lair. Then he finally pointed out how that could be taken—my Lady Lair —which became a whole new joke, but only in private, of course. Now I can't ever hear the word *lair* without laughing.

"No. Why?" Tristan asks.

"It's surrounded. It appears you have a fae problem."

Well, shit.

We flash to the far side of the lake as to not annoy the dragon any further, although I'm annoyed myself that he obviously knows we have a problem but refuses to help. I'm starting to think Aidan might have been right all this time, after all, that the dragons don't give a single damn about us.

Vanessa and I stay with the twins while Owen and Tristan flash closer to The Loft to see what Ethan means.

"Uh, Mom?" Brielle whispers from behind me shortly after they leave, a catch to her voice.

When I turn around, I find a horde of zombies headed our way. Unlike those in movies of the past, our zombies don't amble along, at least, not the newer ones. They run, and they're making a beeline straight for us.

And the day just keeps getting better and better.

Elli instantly reveals her wings. "Come on. We got this, Brie. They hate fire, remember?"

They lift into the air, and each of them blasts a stream of flames at the sprinting corpses. The first several rows go down, but more just run over the fallen.

"Take them from the back," I tell the girls as Vanessa and I sprint toward the front of the horde, weapons drawn.

We eliminate them all, killing them for good, within minutes, but we've barely given each other a nod of celebration when five Demons soar toward the girls, who are still in the air. My wings burst free, and I spring up, flying right past the twins.

"Get to the ground," I order.

"Hell no!" Elliana replies with the first hint of joy I've heard or seen from her since Dani left.

Brielle drops to the ground, knowing she's not needed. I sigh when Elli doesn't. "Aim for their throats, then."

"I know what I'm doing." And she does. She decapitates two with one swipe of her sword, and before I finish with the two closest to me, she's ended a third one's existence in this world.

"Nice job," I say, and she allows a grin to briefly grace her face. "But if you ever want to be on my elite squad, you better learn how to take orders. 'Hell no' is not the proper response to your commander."

She frowns. "I thought you were just being my mom."

"Does it matter?" I challenge, and she doesn't answer me. She knows the right answer, but won't admit it. Always stubborn, that one.

By the time we return to the ground, Owen and Tristan are back.

"We definitely have a fae problem," Tristan says. "Both light and dark. They're just sniffing around, watching the area. It doesn't seem that they can see The Loft through the wards, but we can't take the chance. Fae magic can trump even Owen's. But there's no doubt what they're looking for."

Glancing at the twins, I push my hand through my hair. "So what do we do?"

"Don't forget we also have a Demon and a Daemoni problem," Vanessa says as she flicks a glob of black Demon blood off her shoulder and into the smoldering pile of burning zombies. As if we need reminding.

"Take them somewhere safe until we figure out a long-term solution," Tristan replies.

But where is safe, if not the beach house and not The Loft? Ravenbury is out, as we aren't about to jeopardize the townsfolk—again. We consider

Amadis Island, but some of our people have begun to rebuild there in the last year or so. It's not properly protected, not like it used to be anyway, and we're not about to bring this problem to the place where they finally feel safe again. I suddenly feel like we've gone back in time, to when Tristan and I were being hunted by the Daemoni. We had airplanes then that took us all around the world, but at least we have portals now.

"I don't think we should go far," I say. "Our people are at The Loft."

Owen creates a portal that takes us to an abandoned town on the far side of The Loft, on the shores of Lake of the Ozarks. It's closer to Misery's Edge, but not too close for comfort. We find what had probably been a beautiful, lakeside house in its day, sitting on a peninsula that creates the end of a deep cove off the winding lake. Now the house is overrun by nature. Owen cloaks the entire peninsula, and we hunker down for the night. I know it's not good for the matriarch to be on the run and can only hope this is a temporary situation. But I'll do what it takes to protect my daughters.

We don't pick up our conversation with the twins where we left off. It's been too insane of a day to focus on it now. I hope the girls at least now understand the real danger they're in, though. The timing couldn't have been much more perfect to drive that point home, and they don't even have their powers yet. I have a feeling Dorian hadn't been exaggerating. Once their powers are restored, there could be all-out war again, if not before.

The next morning, Elliana and I go down to the lake shore to collect water for her and Brielle to purify. Brie and Tristan stay up at the house, trying to figure out if they can get the house's solar battery pack to hold any kind of charge. Vanessa and Owen have returned to The Loft to check on things and bring us back some food.

"Brielle thinks you know how to break the curse on us," Elli says almost nonchalantly as she squats down in front of the lapping waves and begins to manipulate a stream of water into the bucket I hold.

"She does?" I ask, my tone careful and cautious to not betray anything. We have a lot more to tell them before we start discussing how to release their full powers.

"It makes sense. It's why you wanted to have the talk yesterday, right?"

"We're not done with that, by the way. There's more you two need to know."

She stands and looks me in the eye. "So when are we going to finish?"

While I gather my thoughts on that, her gaze flickers over my shoulder, and her mouth drops open. "No. Way."

Then she takes off in a sprint.

"Elliana!" I hiss as I whirl around, but it's too late. She's already beyond the cloak's boundaries.

And I see why: Dani walks along the shore around the side of the cove.

# CHAPTER 6

So much for the lesson I'd hoped the girls had learned yesterday. Elliana runs for Dani like she has no cares in the world, and I brace myself for the drama that's about to ensue. Except there isn't any—Dani throws her arms open and swallows Elli in a hug.

"Oh my gosh, I'm so sorry!" she says, kissing the side of Elli's head while they still embrace. "I left Papa as soon as he was settled in Misery's Edge to come back for you."

"I knew you wouldn't leave me." Elli steps back, finally releasing the other woman. "Come on!" Grabbing Dani's hand, she turns and tugs her back toward me. Dani's body gives a small shudder when they pass through the wards.

"Whoa! I didn't see you there, Alexis," she says. "Oh, wow—or that house."

Elli laughs—*laughs*. "That's Owen's doing. He has us cloaked." I give Elliana a look, and she rolls her eyes, but adds, "We're just being cautious. We sleep better with it."

"What are you even doing here, though?" Dani asks. "I thought you lived closer to Ravenbury."

"That's a long story." And despite my visual warning, Elli tells her about the attacks.

"You should come to Misery's Edge with me," Dani says when she's done.

"Definitely," Elli immediately agrees.

I shake my head. "We can't. They don't allow supernaturals there. They especially don't like us."

Dani's dark eyes squint. "But there's all kinds there. I don't know if any live there—we haven't been there long enough—but they definitely trade at the market."

"Really?" I ask in true surprise. "Ranker allows that?"

"I don't know who Ranker is," she says with a shrug, "but Camila doesn't have a problem with supernaturals."

"Who's Camila?"

"Papa's friend. She's the new mayor."

My interest is piqued, and I straighten. "A new mayor in Misery's Edge?"

Dani nods. "Sí. We've only been there a few days, but her recent takeover is all anybody can talk about. She's like me—human, but ... different now."

I turn back toward the lake, gazing across it but not really seeing it as my mind churns over this new information.

"I guess it makes sense," I murmur, wondering if it's true. If so, it might change everything.

"She says she kind of met you during the war. She was in AK's Angels in DC?"

Hmm ... that would mean she might have fought for me, too. But I don't remember meeting a Camila, and she obviously hadn't come to The Loft with the others. Of course, not all of AK's Angels had come to The Loft. They'd scattered for whatever shelter they could find when the bombs began to drop. I wonder if Carlie remembers her. She must have stood out, if she had this kind of leadership ability at the time—it wouldn't have been easy for her to overthrow Ranker. This could be a new ally for us. Definitely a game-changer.

"So we can go to Misery's Edge now!" Elliana's excitement bubbles over, and I begin to think our warnings yesterday have fallen on deaf ears.

I should probably tell Dani to leave—there's too much risk being with us—but she is safe within the cloak and I can't bring myself to hurt Elli again.

"*Tristan?*" I mentally call out.

"*I heard the whole thing,*" he replies from inside the house, and I'm grateful for his superior hearing.

"*Do you remember a Camila?*"

"*No, but we didn't meet every single person on that campus while we were there.*" Very true—we'd been a little preoccupied at the time. "*Even if I did, though, I don't think it should change anything. Going to Misery's Edge is not the best solution for anybody.*"

"*What do we do about Dani?*"

There's a beat of silence. "*Sorry, can't hear you. Brielle's calling for me.*"

I internally roll my eyes. "*Tristan?*" He doesn't reply. "*Calling on my second in command!*"

"*Yes, boss?*" his mental voice teases.

"*Dani?*" I silently growl.

"*No good solutions there.*"

Yeah, no kidding. Risk the woman's life or break my daughter's heart —again? Of course, I'm pretty sure Elliana wouldn't let that happen. No, if I make Dani leave, Elli will absolutely go with her, especially now that she's heard Dani's explanation—and even more especially now that she thinks she's allowed within the walls of Misery's Edge, a place she's only heard stories about and has always wanted to see.

When I realize the pair have been quiet, I turn back to them to ensure they haven't run off. Elliana sits by herself on the rocky shore, no Dani to be seen.

"Did Dani leave?" I ask.

Elli looks up and smiles—a real smile, which is a rarity. "She'll be back."

"Where'd she go?"

"I don't know. My stomach growled obnoxiously loud, and I told her we didn't have any food. She had an idea and said she'd be back in about fifteen minutes." She gives a little shrug, her normal intensity gone.

My brows lower as a feeling of unease slithers across my shoulders. The girl knows where we are and then takes off?

"*Tristan, I think we need to go.*"

"*Without Scarecrow?*"

Crap. He's right. No Owen means no portal, which means, whether we fly or walk, we'd still be without a cloak. If every evil faction in the multiverse weren't after my daughters, I wouldn't care. We could handle ourselves. But I'm not about to risk them.

"*At least come out here with us?*" I ask Tristan. If Dani brings back an army of Daemoni or Demons or fae or whatever, I don't want Tristan even a flash away. I want him by my side.

He and Brielle join us by the water a second later. While the girls huddle together, playing with magic, Tristan and I stay on edge, constantly scanning the area and watching the skies, waiting for any sign of an attack. I silently curse my protector for not returning yet while I also pray that nothing has happened to him. That he didn't try to stop whatever hunts us, whatever might be heading our way this very minute, on his own.

"There's Dani," Elli says after more like thirty minutes than fifteen. She jumps to her feet and points at a place about a quarter of a mile away, on the opposite shore. "Someone's with her."

Tristan and I both drop into defensive stance, weapons drawn. Dani and a woman stand near a copse of trees, Dani gesturing around the lake. The other woman, dressed in a plain brown top, blue jeans, and knee-high boots, is strikingly beautiful with straight, glossy black hair that falls in waves over her shoulders and almond-shaped dark eyes that sweep the area, following Dani's hand. Her tanned complexion is so smooth, she seems timeless, but at the same time, something about her makes me think she's quite a bit more mature than Dani, perhaps even middle-aged.

"They can see me?" the woman asks Dani, her voice smooth as honey.

"I'm sure they can."

We can not only see her but easily hear her, too, with our inhuman senses.

"Very good. That's all I need. Thank you, Daniela. I hope to see you home soon." Then in a blur, the woman runs away.

I stiffen again, wondering where she's gone. Whom she might be bringing back. After a few minutes, Dani disappears too. A moment later, a fast-moving blur comes to a halt in the same place Elli had spotted her earlier this morning. She looks around, her brows furrowing as though she's confused.

"Seriously, parents?" Elli asks when she looks over at us, weapons out and ready to fight, before walking to the edge of the cloak's boundary where Dani is. My heart skips a beat when she steps out but it's only long enough to grab Dani's hand before she hurries back in, Dani in tow.

"Oh, good," Dani breathes. "I was hoping I was in the right spot. The cloak is … disorienting." She looks over at Tristan and me. "Did you get a good look at Camila?"

"The woman who was with you? Where did she go?" I demand.

"Back to Misery's Edge. That's what took so long—she insisted on talking with you, but I wasn't about to bring her straight to you. I trust her, but I don't want to piss you off. So she thought maybe if you just saw her face, you'd remember. She also wanted me to give you this." Dani reached into her backpack and pulled out four sandwiches, as well as a piece of folded paper. She handed a sandwich and the paper to me before handing out the rest of the food.

When I unfolded the paper, an old, faded photograph fell out.

"That's definitely Carlie." Tristan points to one of the young women in the photo. The blonde with the sweet, girl-next-door features looks just like I remember her from my own college days, only a few years older. "And next to her is the woman we just saw. Camila."

"Hmm ... so you think she's telling the truth?"

"Read the note."

*Alexis & Tristan,*

*I don't know if you remember me, so I thought the photograph might help. We never actually met, but because of my assistance to Carlie, your friend Sheree is still alive. I am on your side. I have people here who fought in the war and will fight to protect your family again. I would love to meet your daughters and hope to see Carlie again too. You can find safe refuge at Misery's Edge, if you would like, but my influence goes far beyond with communities from here to New Orleans. We can be strong allies, which I think you can use right now. It is your decision, but for you, our gates are open.*

*Regards,*

*Camila, Mayor of Misery's Edge*

"What do you think?" I ask Tristan as we sit.

He's smelling all of the sandwiches before deeming them safe to eat and holds a piece he's torn off to Sasha. "I think it's okay, but what do you think, girl? Is it safe?"

Sasha sniffs the food, cautious at first, but then nearly bites off his finger to take it.

"Guess we're not the only ones who are hungry," Tristan mutters as the girls laugh. We watch the *lykora* for a minute or two. "It's safe?"

Sasha dips her head in a nod, and Tristan doles out the sandwiches again. I watch Dani, but she doesn't seem offended by our suspicion.

She'd taken precautions with Camila, not giving away our exact location, and allowing enough time to pass for the mayor to be far gone before she headed this way. Of course, Camila could have always returned to follow, but so far, it seems like Dani had done all she could to protect us—and feed us.

"I mean, what do you think about Camila and Misery's Edge?" I ask Tristan.

He swallows the bite he's just taken. "She's right that we need allies."

"So you think we can trust her? What happened to Misery's Edge not being the best solution?"

"I wouldn't say we can trust her, but it might not hurt to arrange for a meeting to see if we can learn more. The more facts I know, the clearer the solution," he reminds me. "We can start by making sure Carlie recognizes her."

I take a bite of the cheese and tomato sandwich, thinking as I chew. "She does know Sheree was dying when we first arrived on that campus, but she could have learned that along the way. What if Carlie doesn't remember her?"

"We should still at least meet with her. Carlie's human with a human memory, so that doesn't necessarily mean anything. And we do need allies, especially one with a vast network of human communities. Lucas threw a lot of obstacles our way when he turned the Normans against us. We can't let that happen again. If she can help with that, then we need to at least give her a chance to prove herself."

He makes a good point, but we don't decide yet. Just as we finish the sandwiches, Owen and Vanessa return, carrying a sack with more food and fresh water, which is good because the girls' magic just isn't enough to purify this lake water. I send Owen back to The Loft one more time to show the picture to Carlie. By the time he returns, night has fallen, bringing much cooler temperatures, and we've retreated inside to sit around the dining table. Owen walks in with Carlie right behind him.

"She insisted that she come," Owen says when I lift my brows.

The doctor gives me a small smile that doesn't quite reach her blue eyes. "Sorry, but I wanted to talk to you about Camila myself."

"So you know her?" I ask.

She nods, pushing a lock of her grayish-blond hair behind her ear before sliding into the chair next to me. "She was two years ahead of me in med school and a mentor. She pushed me hard, but for my own good.

She might be the most brilliant scientist I've ever met. She'd earned a full scholarship that brought her to DC all the way from humble beginnings in the mountains of Brazil."

"That would explain her connection to Miguel," I say.

"Yes, she was from the next town over from Papa's home, where I was born," Dani speaks up from across the room where she and the twins sit. I thought they'd been engrossed in their conversation, but of course this would have their interest piqued. "Papa's known her since they were young. When she left for university in America, she told him he could always find her if he ever needed anything. That's why we traveled for years to get here."

Tristan and I exchange a look. The evidence is piling up that this Camila is practically an angel herself and her offer just might be legit. So why does it feel like it's too good to be true?

"I say we go to the Edge and sooner rather than later," Owen says. "We can take an entourage of your strongest—me and Vanessa, Sheree and Aidan, Jax and Charleigh. She and Sasha can protect the twins while we meet with this Camila chick."

"We kind of need Charleigh at The Loft right now," Carlie says. "She and Blossom are our best potion-makers for healing. Besides, I thought you said she's helping fortify the wards on The Loft."

Owen scrubs a hand through his straw-colored hair. "Right." He nods, but then shrugs. "We'll be fine, though. The town's mostly human, right? How bad can it get? And the twins aren't exactly defenseless."

"Hold up," I say. "Why does The Loft need so much medical attention and fortified wards? What haven't you told me?"

Carlie shrinks back, her bottom lip pulling down. "Oops," she murmurs as Owen gives her the stink eye.

"Owen?" I prod.

"The fae are still surrounding the area," he finally replies. "I don't know if some of them can see through our cloak or if they're just wandering a little too close in by sheer dumb luck, but we're not taking any chances. So far, it seems that only lesser fae have been sent, but if they discover one little clue, stronger ones could be there in a heartbeat. The Demons also seem to be homing in on us, coming much closer than ever before. We're taking precautions, but you don't need to worry. I'm sure they'll be distracted soon enough."

"Crap," I mutter. With my elbows on the table, I massage my temples.

Things seem to be escalating so quickly. I look over at the girls, who are playing a card game with an old deck they found stashed in a drawer. We might need to break the spell, whether we're ready or not, just so they have a fighting chance. I turn my gaze on Tristan, who sits next to me, and it feels like we fall right into our own little world. "We're running out of time, aren't we?"

"It seems that way, *ma lykita*," he murmurs, leaning forward and brushing a stray hair off my cheek. "Let's go to Misery's Edge tomorrow and meet with this Camilla. If we can form an alliance, then we can buy ourselves some time to prepare the girls properly before shit hits the fan."

Knowing I need to trust in him and my other advisors, I exhale slowly before turning back to the rest of the table. "Owen, gather the others in the morning. Not just Sheree, Aidan, and Jax, either. I want a small army."

I wish Ragan and her hunter team were available, but they're on another trip down south, still trying to find her original master-teacher—that old woman in the bayou who'd created the hunters. Previous searches had brought them back empty-handed, and we'd all but given up on the chance that she was still alive, but then James, of all people, stumbled upon another clue of where to find her. We need any information she knows about Demons now more than ever.

"I'm going, too," Carlie pipes up.

"The hell you are," I say.

"You're walking into a town that has been nothing but humans for over a decade. You need Norman representation," she points out. "Who better than a kind, compassionate, harmless doctor, especially since I have a close relationship with their leader?"

My nose scrunches as I look at Tristan. He nods, agreeing with her. I'm not too keen on the idea of having someone so vulnerable to protect if everything goes badly.

"Trust in your people," Tristan reminds me later that night when I can't sleep. "Trust in *yourself*."

I swallow and press into his side as his arm wraps around me. He's right, of course. Hadn't I told myself the same thing earlier? *This is the Age of Angels. This is my time. We will be fine.* I repeat that to myself until sleep finally comes.

Later the next morning, we all stand on a hill under a magical cloak, scoping out the town below on the banks of the Mississippi River.

Misery's Edge is now bigger than it had been in the Before time, when it wasn't much more than a gas stop near the intersection of the highway to St. Louis and another crossing the river. The town is now comprised of concentric circles, like a massive target. At its center, right off Main Street where maybe the town park had been, is a large area of tables surrounded by makeshift walls of fabric or plywood, covered by tarps and tattered sheets—the bustling marketplace.

Many of the brick buildings on the two-block long Main Street still stand, but not many of the houses. They've been replaced by structures comprised of an eclectic collection of repurposed materials, from tin to wood to concrete blocks, that butt up against each other and what remains of the buildings. Two rows of these encircle the center with alleys that cross through them, like spokes in a wheel. Then there are several rows of objects brought in to provide more housing—railroad cars, semi-trailers, even grain silos. A wall made of corrugated metal surrounds the entire town, which they've had to move back and add on to with each new row of housing. It's obvious the town has physically grown outward as its population has increased over the years.

There are four breaks in the outer walls—one in each compass direction—with metal gates stretched across them. A half-dozen heavily armed guards stand at each one, and I wonder how they make the ammunition for all the guns they sport. More guards squat along the tops of the walls, just behind the coils of razor wire that line the edges.

"I promise you have nothing to worry about," Dani says, standing on the other side of Elliana, who's right next to me. "Camila is special. If you don't trust me or Papa, at least trust your own doctor and friend."

Not wanting to delay this any longer, I give the signal to drop the cloak—and pray to the Angels that I'm not about to make the worst mistake of my life.

Too bad they're not listening anymore.

# CHAPTER 7

*A*lthough we've been invited, I still hold my breath as our large group approaches the western gate. I really don't want to have to fight with humans. My purpose is to do the opposite—to protect them. But I also won't let them hurt my people and especially not my daughters. We're obviously recognized and expected, though, because the gate opens and the guards part without a word exchanged. When I check their minds, not a single threatening or even disparaging thought can be heard. In fact, their thoughts are all mundane and boring, worried about everyday life such as what they're going to eat for their next meal or whose arms they'd like to find comfort in tonight. I let loose my breath, but that's about as far as I can go to relax. I can't pinpoint it, but something feels just a little bit ... off.

Camila stands about thirty yards beyond the gate, in the middle of the spoke that leads to the center of town. Owen and Vanessa, who lead the way in front of Tristan and me, separate when we get close, allowing Tristan and me to step forward, Carlie coming up to my other side. Everyone else falls into form behind us, surrounding the twins and Dani.

"Alexis Ames, I presume," Camila says, her gaze trained on me the entire time until we reach her.

"Alexis Ames Knight," I correct. "And you must be Camila."

She dips her head before acknowledging Tristan and then smiles widely at Carlie, who formally introduces us.

"And now that the formalities are done ..." Camila rushes over to Carlie, and the two embrace each other.

Carlie's the first to step back, and I don't know if anyone else notices or if I'm being extra sensitive, but the way she moves is almost like she's trying to escape something uncomfortable.

*"Everything okay?"* I silently ask her.

*"Huh? Oh, yeah, fine. She's just a little ... different than I remember her. She looks almost the exact same, but feels different, if that makes sense. Of course, a lot has happened in the eighteen years since I've seen her, including the end of the world."* She pauses then adds, *"But it's really not fair that I'm the only person I know who's aging normally. She's older than me, but I practically look like her grandma!"*

One corner of my mouth lifts slightly in a smile before I remember that we're having a private conversation. I don't want to look like I'm smirking at anything Camila is saying—which, turns out, is also about age.

"Your daughters could be your sisters," Camila says, peering over my shoulder. She shakes her head. "Such a strange world we live in now." She holds out her hand, addressing the twins with a warm smile. When she does, I notice fine lines around her eyes and the corners of her mouth. She's definitely not forever-young like some of us, but simply aging well. In fact, upon closer inspection, I might say she's late thirties or early forties, a little closer to expectations than I'd thought on my first impression out by the lake. "I'm Camila. You must be Brielle, and you must be Elliana." She nails their names, which is a little surprising considering some people at The Loft still can't tell them apart. "Daniela has told me all about you."

Tristan and I part so the girls can shake her hand. Throughout all of this, part of my mind continues sweeping the area, listening to nearby thoughts. A few people here are excited by our presence in a good way, and the rest couldn't care less as they go about their daily lives. Still, I can't seem to find comfort in that.

"Welcome to Misery's Edge," Camila says to all of us, her gaze traveling over our entire group before coming back to me. "I am glad you took me up on my offer, but you didn't need to bring an army."

Her tone is teasing so I smile, but she's not wrong. In addition to most of my core council, besides Blossom and Ragan, Owen brought a dozen of our own guards with us.

"The former regime here has not been kind to our people," Tristan says. "You can understand our need for caution."

"Of course, of course." Camila waves a hand in the air. "I was only teasing. But Ranker works for me now and has been re-educated about the supernaturals."

Tristan and I exchange a glance. What the hell does that mean—re-educated?

"He won't be a problem for you any longer," she adds. "Now come, let's walk. Let me show you around this little town that thrives like no others within a three-hundred-mile radius."

"So I have to know," I say as we begin walking down the roadway toward the center of town, trying to keep my tone as light as hers and not betray my suspicions. "How the heck did you defeat Ranker and become mayor?"

Camila chuckles as she falls into step between Carlie and me. "Not easily—at first, anyway. I've been helping trading towns establish and grow across the south. When the bombs started dropping and everyone scattered, I missed Carlie's group when they left, so another took me in because of my medical training. We found shelter in a government facility south of Washington and stayed there for a few years before we dared to don the hazmat suits because we were getting desperate for supplies. When we discovered the air and ground was tainted more by magic than by nuclear fallout, we took our chances. Long story short, my services were needed in many of the emerging communities, so I traveled a lot. I began to see the need for a trading network among them and led the way to make that happen."

She shrugs as though it's no big deal, but I'd heard about the efforts, without knowing her specific involvement. There had been times those communities came to the verge of battling each other for resources before they were able to see how they could help each other. Each time, we'd prepared to step in, but it never became necessary. It seems I have Camila to thank for that—if she speaks the truth. Which I just can't tell.

That feeling that something is the slightest bit off here remains. No, it grows. Not just with her but with the whole town. I can't pinpoint the sensation, though. It's like when a foul odor lingers even after the source of it has been long removed, probably only noticeable to the most sensitive. I'd like to think it's the residual stink of Ranker and his bigoted, misogynistic, close-minded men, but I'm just not sure.

"Anyway, Misery's Edge is in a prime location and was doing great on its own, which we all know," Camila continues. "But I knew Ranker was not the person who could lead this important town to its full potential. This became especially apparent the last year or two, as things seem to have been shifting across the region." She tilts her head, peering sideways at me. "The supernatural communities have been more on edge. The humans, as well, but they don't know why. I know. Of course, you do as well."

Although I watch ahead as we pass by a row of housing, I turn more of my attention on her, trying to prod her mind. I can't really pick up on anything more than what she's saying out loud. What, exactly, does she know? What, exactly, is she hiding?

"I've felt that energy shift, that feeling of darkness, growing for years," she says. "One of my new abilities, maybe. I know whatever it is has the supers especially riled up, and your family seems to be at the center of it once again. The dynamics have changed, though, even among the humans, haven't they?" she asks rhetorically. "Take Dani and me and those like us, for instance. We are not supernatural, but how long before people start accusing us of not being human either? People like Ranker and his followers. With his position against all supernaturals, I knew he'd do more harm than good for this town, if things escalate. Which it seems they are now. It only took a little convincing of the townspeople for them to realize he was a shit leader."

I laugh. Now that I can agree on.

We come upon the first row of shops that outlines the edge of the marketplace square, and the girls grow loud with excited chatter as they take it all in. It's no more than a flea market of the Before time, but it's their era's equivalent to a small shopping center or large box store, and they're seeing such a place for the first time ever. We explore for a while with Camila's guidance, stopping at booths and meeting merchants who sell everything from leather scraps to dried meat to scavenged technology, which catches Brielle's full attention. She and Tristan both linger at that booth while I move a little closer to where Elliana and Dani have drifted, to a shop where a woman not much older than them sells clothing.

"What do you have to trade?" the woman asks Elli when her finger drifts carefully over a beautiful red silk top with orange and yellow stitching that gives the appearance of flames dancing along the hem.

Elli looks over at me with a plea in her eyes. I give a small shake of my head.

"*Why not?*" she asks, taking advantage of my telepathy because it suits her.

"*I know it's pretty, but it has no place in our world. Where would you wear it?*"

"*Do I need a reason to appreciate something beautiful? Why can't I just wear it at home?*"

I don't remind her that we don't even know if we have a home right now. "*We have nothing to trade. Everything on us is highly valuable.*"

"Thread? Fabric?" the woman asks as her gaze drifts over my daughter's fighting leathers. "That corset would do."

Elliana's hand darts from the red silk to her own top, and she laughs, understanding what I mean now. "This is no ordinary leather. I don't think your entire inventory is worth this."

The woman frowns, and I quickly steer the girls away before we can offend her any further. Not that Elli is wrong. Our leathers are enchanted, as are our weapons. They're one-of-a-kind and priceless. And they're the only items we have on us, perhaps all we might own for the foreseeable future. As we walk back to Tristan and Brielle, I glance over my shoulder at the red blouse and hate that we're in a position where I can't provide a little treat for my daughter.

We turn the corner of the market square, and Camila points out a couple of booths, one showcasing an eclectic collection of herbs and stones and the other bottles of what is no doubt blood.

"They are our newest additions as we try to integrate the supernatural community," the mayor explains. "We hope that section grows as more of your kind feel welcome here."

"Whoa," Carlie breathes from just behind me, her attention on a very different shop that's bigger than the others. "Is that fresh gauze?"

"That and much more," Camila says with a smile, and the two hurry over to investigate.

Fifteen minutes later, Carlie and Sheree are loaded down with medical supplies.

"How?" I ask.

"My gift to Carlie," Camila replies, "and to you and your people. A gesture of goodwill."

"Oh, wow, I'm so grateful, but I'm sure we don't need—"

"Yes, we do," Carlie jumps in.

"Yes, you do," Camila says at the same time. "We have more, and Carlie says your people need it. Allow me this gesture of kindness. I know you will be able to repay in other ways."

She closes her hand over my forearm in what is probably meant to be reassuring, but I feel a thread of something not kind or generous and definitely not comforting. A reminder, I presume, that nothing in life is ever truly free.

"We need to get this home A.S.A.P.," Carlie says. "Do you mind taking Sheree and me back, Owen?"

Owen looks at me with a brow raised. A sense of foreboding dances along the small of my back—a niggling feeling that our sworn protector shouldn't be leaving right now. On the other hand, he should only be gone for less than an hour, and we still have Vanessa, Aidan, and Jax here, and, of course, Tristan and myself.

"I'll stay," Sheree says, shifting the weight of the boxes she holds. "Owen can take these."

I glance over at the girls, where they stand on the corner, joined by Dani's father. They smile and giggle at whatever he's saying. Then I look at Tristan.

"*We'll be fine for an hour,*" he assures, practically rolling his eyes. I hope this means he doesn't feel what I do, that I'm letting my fear get the best of me. I'd promised myself long ago to stop acting out of fear and instead live out of love.

"We'll see you in about an hour, Owen," I say.

Nodding, he takes the boxes from Sheree, and he and Carlie stroll back down the spoke that leads to the gate out of town.

"Mom," Brielle says, suddenly at my side, "Dani wants to show us her new home. Miguel's made lunch. Is that okay?"

"I think it's time we talk business anyway," Camila says.

The unease in my belly grows stronger. I don't like that we're all scattering now. I've been able to manage my paranoia when my people have remained close by me, just knowing those I trust most are nearby, plus giving us strength in numbers. Like a mama bird, I want to keep them all, but especially our most vulnerable, under my wings.

Now I almost feel like someone is trying to divide and conquer.

# CHAPTER 8

*C*amila gestures at the four-story brick building behind us that appears as though it was once for government use, which I suppose makes sense.

"We'll be right in there, and Miguel lives right over there, in the corner of that building." She points to another structure left from the Before time, just across the street. "Still in your sight line."

That does make me feel a little better, so I give my consent, sending Sheree and Aidan along with the twins. We can't be too complacent now, not when it all seems too good to be true. Usually that means it is.

With Vanessa and Jax at our sides and the rest of our entourage right behind us, Tristan and I follow Camila to Misery's Edge's town hall. I give silent orders to the guards to remain outside at the door as Vanessa, Jax, Tristan, and I continue into the building. There's a small lobby that reaches to the back of the structure, with stairs climbing the sides of each wall to either side of the entry. Just beyond the stairs are hallways in each direction. Camila turns right, leading us down one of them.

"Misery's Edge was once the county seat, so this building is larger than what we need now. The upstairs offices have been converted into barracks and small apartments," Camila explains. "If you choose to stay, we can put your family up there until we can make room elsewhere. I imagine you'd want your guards close by, too."

I almost correct her to say council, but change my mind. She can go on believing they're here for protection and not also because they have the highest authority among the Amadis. If something should happen to Tristan and me—or my girls—a real army would be here in no time.

"That's quite generous of you," I say. "But we should discuss all of that first."

"Exactly," Camila responds, finally stopping at the last door before another stairwell. "My office."

When we step in, I nearly stumble in surprise. I'd expected something along the lines of my modest office back at The Loft, but this is more like the luxurious one Rina used to have at the Amadis mansion. The one I'd only been able to enjoy for a few short weeks before all Hell broke loose. Large, heavy wood furniture fills the broad space—a polished credenza with an executive desk squatting in front of it, a leather chair between them. Two guest chairs sit on this side of the desk. The walls to our left are lined with bookcases, a leather couch sitting on an ornate rug between them.

"I have a feeling Ranker never touched a single one of those," Camila remarks as my gaze slides over the books on the shelves, and I laugh. Partly because I know it's true, and partly because it explains the decadence of the office. Of course Ranker would keep this all to himself rather than allowing any of it to be repurposed in a number of ways that could serve a lot of people. She slips behind the desk and gives me a pointed look. "Just us?"

I glance over my shoulder at Vanessa and Jax who have stepped inside the room. When I give them a nod, Vanessa scowls, but follows Jax back out to the hall, closing the door behind her.

"*If this all goes badly, that Camila chick is* mine," Vanessa says, and the way she says that last word reminds me of years ago when she'd claimed me in the same way. "*Something's just rubbing me the wrong way with her, which is bugging the shit out of me.*"

I'm kind of glad to hear her suspicions. I feel less paranoid now. Or, at least, more justified for it.

"*Listen to what you can hear from others,*" I tell her. "*And don't block me out!*"

"*Yes, boss.*" She says it almost with sincerity, which puts me even more on edge, especially when I feel her mind completely open to mine. That's not something she likes to do, although she has grown more trusting of me over the years. It's taken this long to prove that I don't prod unless it's necessary.

"So," Camilla begins as we all sit, and she leans back in her chair. "I offered you refuge here in my town. I do think my people and yours could make an alliance that would be mutually beneficial. But before we work out those details, I need to know the facts. I know what I've heard, but I don't know what's actually true. What exactly is going on?"

I lean a little closer to Tristan, who sits in the chair next to me, and study the woman in front of us. "What *do* you know? What have you heard?"

She eyes me back, and I wonder if we've already hit an impasse. "I've heard the Daemoni and the Demons are both preparing for another war. I've heard the fae are coming to our world in numbers unseen since before humans ever existed here. I've heard that your family is at the center of it all—specifically, your daughters."

So she's heard a lot of what Dorian told us the other day. A lot more than I expected.

When we don't reply, she calls us out. "Your silence speaks volumes. It is all true then?"

"We don't know any more than you, it seems," Tristan says easily, calmly. "The Daemoni's attempts to claim the Amadis daughters have been on-going for millennia, so it's really just status quo."

Her head cocks as she studies him. "Is it, though? I think it's more. The Demons and the fae are involved, too. Even some of the human factions around the world. They *all* want your daughters. Why? What exactly can they do?"

He shrugs, but I can feel in him the same tension coiling in my muscles. A protectiveness for our daughters keeps a tight hold on any answers we might have that go beyond the obvious, vague ones. I'm absolutely not about to tell her or anyone what exactly they can do.

I straighten in my seat, pulling my shoulders back and lifting my chin. "The Daemoni have always wanted the Amadis daughters because we are powerful. The other factions know that now, as well. Our daughters are hovering that line between innocence and maturity, which makes their potential exciting and their vulnerability tempting. Now more than ever, they're seen as objects to be owned. I would think, as a woman, you would understand that's reason enough—and not at all okay."

Camila nods, as though agreeing, but then she leans forward, folding her hands on her desk. "Look. I understand your need to keep your secrets in the interest of your daughters' safety, but consider my perspective. I'm offering to take you in at the risk of attracting the attention of entities far more powerful than my people. I think it's only fair that I know what we're protecting."

I sit back, pretending to consider this, but already knowing my answer.

"*She's right,*" I say to Tristan.

"*She is.*"

"*So we're done here?*"

"*We are.*"

"It *is* only fair," I agree with Camila, and she smiles, but then it falters when I stand. "So it's probably best that we don't stay. Your offer is generous, but it's too risky."

"We don't want to be responsible for anything happening to your people because of us," Tristan clarifies.

"My people are well prepared for what it means for you to be here—the risks as well as the rewards. We believe your presence would be mutually beneficial. I just want to know *why*—the reason for taking these risks."

My eyes narrow. "Is Misery's Edge in danger? Do you need protection? My understanding is you're safer without us."

"Most likely, yes, but nothing is guaranteed. And *you* need allies," she says as she stands to meet my gaze, an urgent edge to her voice that almost sounds like desperation or frustration. "Surely you must realize that!"

"*Does she sound like she's hiding something to you?*" I ask Tristan.

"*Definitely. As though she needs us here more than we need to be here.*"

"*I don't like it.*"

"*Neither do I, ma lykita. We need to get out of here.*"

"Yes, you're right again," I say to Camila, keeping my voice calm and clear. "And we would love to have the humans as our allies. After all, the Amadis are theirs—always have been, always will be, regardless of what they choose. But at the end of the war, when the last of the Angels left, they gave me one final message."

Pushing the chair back with my heel so as not to knock it over, I reveal my wings, reminding her who—what—I am. I lift them so they arch high over my head, the tips barely brushing the ground. The golden afternoon sunlight streaming through the dirty window makes the purple gleam like an iridescent shine over the black. Leaning forward and placing my hands on her desk, I draw on their strength to deliver my next words.

"This is the Age of Angels. This is *our* time to rule, and I have complete faith we will conquer evil once again." I see a flicker of something in her eyes, but when I try to read her thoughts, I get nothing. "I hope we *can* be allies, Camila. I hope we can fight together again for what is right, if it comes to that, which I sincerely hope it does not. But I will not for one minute jeopardize my daughters or the humans." I lean back and hide my wings. "So in that spirit, we say thank you for your hospitality, but we graciously decline."

I turn for the door, Tristan right behind me.

"Think about it," Camila calls after us. "Talk to your daughters—they might want differently." This causes me to pause at the door, because I know she is right. Elliana, at least, will want to stay. "The sun will set soon. Why don't you stay here for the night and sleep on it? You can give me your final decision in the morning."

As I open the door, I look over my shoulder and dip my chin. "Thank you, again."

I stride out of the office and down the hall with purpose, Tristan by my side and Jax and Vanessa falling in behind us.

"*That was badass, sister,*" Vanessa says as we head out of the lobby, which makes me internally smile. She rarely doles out any kind of praise, especially to me. As my older half-sister, she's constantly challenging me to become better and stronger, which I appreciate. Still, I can't help but feel a little warm inside with the compliment. "*Wish I could have seen the look on her face when you showed your wings.*"

"*How do you know I showed my wings?*" I'm not at all surprised she heard the whole exchange, but I didn't know my wings make a sound when they appear.

"*I can smell it. Kind of like baby powder.*"

"*You've never mentioned that before! Wait—you mean like Sasha?*"

"*More like Sasha's breath,*" she quips.

As I try to think of a retort, I consider what Sasha's breath smells like. "*I'll take that as a compliment.*"

Vanessa snorts out loud. I know she can't mind the scent too much, because she's always eager to drink from my vein whenever I allow it, wings out or not.

The rest of our group follows as we cross the street to gather the girls so we can leave as soon as Owen returns, hopefully before nightfall. I have no intention of sleeping on her offer. We don't belong here, and the sooner we leave, the better for everyone. I brace myself, knowing we're in for a big fight from at least one of my daughters.

Unfortunately, I don't expect Miguel to greet us, and I just can't bring myself to argue with the older man.

"You stay for dinner, yes?" he asks, his English still broken and heavily accented but already better than it had been just two weeks ago. As if on cue, my stomach growls and my mouth salivates at the scents permeating the smoke that drifts from around the corner of his home—garlic, onion, meat, and something else that seems vaguely familiar. I'm pretty sure I haven't smelled such a medley of flavors since the Before time.

"I don't—" I start, but I'm interrupted.

"We're making *feijoada*," Sheree calls from somewhere to our right. She pokes her head from around the corner of the building. "A Brazilian black bean and pork stew. They even have chorizo!"

We walk around to find an area of cracked cement that had probably been the building's parking lot, but now serves as a patio. Sheree returns to a huge pot that looks almost like a cauldron sitting over a large fire pit in the center of the space and uses a spoon the size of a paddle to stir. Tristan actually groans out loud when we take a peek at the contents. I honestly can't blame him.

"Got a little drool there, mate," Jax teases, wiping his thumb across the corner of his own mouth.

"Can't blame him," Aidan says from above. I crane my neck back to see him standing on the roof of the two-story building next door, his gaze constantly sweeping the area.

"There's enough for us all," Sheree says. "I'd hate to disappoint Miguel, Alexis. He's put so much into this."

I can't believe even Sheree is ganging up on me. On the other hand, Owen still hasn't returned, and without Owen, we have no portal, which wouldn't matter for those of us who can flash, but I'm not about to leave anybody behind. I look over at Vanessa, the only one not drooling, but she only shrugs. As a vampire, she still eats human food and enjoys it, but it doesn't have quite the same appeal as it does to us.

"Fine," I finally agree, ignoring the little voice of fear poking at the back of my mind. My people deserve this, and maybe it will help things go smoother with Elliana if she gets a little more time with Dani. "We'll stay just for dinner, but I'm telling on all of you to Blossom."

Stepping back, Jax throws his hands in the air. "Whoa. Hold on a minute. Leave me out of it, princess. I beg you."

I laugh. "So you don't want any *feijoada*?"

One hand rises higher, skimming over the top of his bald head as his brown gaze looks longingly at the pot. "I didn't say that now, did I?"

Everyone begins setting up makeshift tables around the concrete slab, and chairs are brought from who knows where, accommodating all of my council and our guards. Night falls by the time we finish devouring the stew that just might be the best thing I've eaten since the Before time, not counting the meal Tristan and I had in that other world. I probably won't tell on everyone to Blossom after all, because I definitely can't admit to this. She's done her best with what we've had available, and I won't take that away from her. But holy shit, was this meal amazing.

While I'm a little worried about Owen, I'm also feeling peculiarly content with my very full belly and the wine that's been broken out just for us. Our family joins Miguel and Dani inside for a bit, the older man sharing more of his stories with my husband in Portuguese.

Their home is small—a tiny living room with an adjacent galley kitchen and a single bedroom—created from the front portion of what had been a boutique shop in the Before time. The store's back storage room is now another apartment for a different family. The living room barely fits a threadbare couch and a chair wide enough for both Dani and Elliana to sit in together, though Elli's practically on Dani's lap. A small cafe table with two chairs is pushed up against the corner in the kitchen, and that's it for furniture. It's homey, though, especially as it's lit only by candlelight, and Miguel seems happy that he's finally found his friend Camila—except for a tiny bit of apprehension and tension I keep sensing as it flits through his mind. When I try to latch onto it, though, it sizzles out.

I find it strange that he hasn't said one word about Camila, as far as I can tell anyway. He'd been searching for her for nearly two decades, and yet she hasn't even joined us for this feast among friends ... supposed friends. My mind starts churning through the day's events, rehashing every word said, revisiting each face we met, trying to pinpoint and grab onto that ever-elusive feeling that something is not quite right. At first, I try to convince myself that it's the energy of a gathering storm in the western sky, sending an electrical charge through the air, but it's more than that. Closer than that.

*Shamara.*

The word pops into my head as a thought, but whose, I can't determine. It's not a familiar voice, yet it is at the same time. Almost like my own mind-voice just tossing that name out into the void as if it should mean something.

"We're not staying, are we?" Brielle asks quietly, interrupting my thoughts. She sits on the couch between Tristan and me, her head leaning against my shoulder.

"No, we're not. It's not safe for us or for the people who call this home."

"I figured. And what about Elliana and Dani?"

I blow out a sigh as I peek over at the couple, the flickering flame of the nearby candle casting a dance of light and shadows on their faces. They're so ridiculously cute together. "I guess if Dani wants to come with us, I can't stop her. I don't know if she'll want to leave her papa, though."

"Poor Elli," Brielle murmurs, and I feel her sincerity. None of us want to see Elliana hurt, but I will break her neck and carry her out of here myself before leaving her. Then Brielle adds, "Poor us who will have to live with her." She stands, and before I can warn her, she says, "Don't worry. I won't be the one to break the news."

I chuckle as she goes over to talk with the pair. Tristan turns toward me, and I notice for the first time that it has quieted on his end of the couch and Miguel is gone.

"No Scarecrow yet?" he asks.

I shake my head. "Where's Miguel?"

"He excused himself for a minute. I presume to use the bathroom."

"*We need to go,*" I say silently, because that paranoia from earlier is sliding up my spine with each passing beat of my heart. That name —*Shamara*—echoes in my mind. Dorian—he'd mentioned a Shamara. And then it all comes to me—

"*Alexis!*" My own name blasts in my head, Owen mentally yelling for me. "*Can you fucking hear me?*"

My breath catches, and I stiffen as my eyes lock with Tristan's. I can't remember the last time I've heard Owen sound like this, and it wipes out everything I'd just been thinking. I open my mind to Tristan, linking the three of us. "*Are you okay?*"

"*I'm almost there. It's a trap! We have to get the girls out of there—now!*"

# CHAPTER 9

*J*umping to my feet, I sense out for Owen's mind signature, finding it rushing toward the town's gates. He continues mind-talking to us, I assume with an explanation, but our connection cuts in and out, and all I catch are Demons, Daemoni, and fae—the interference comes from a dark energy settling over the town. No . . . not settling. Zinging through the air, like an electric current, zapping from home to home, the smell of brimstone and sulfur riding on it.

*"Brielle, Elliana, we need to flash!"* I yell into their minds. *"Don't even argue. Just hurry!"* I throw a hand out to each of them to ensure they follow my flash and don't decide to stay, especially Elliana.

But when we try to flash, we can't. It's like smashing into a wall—a solid, black wall of dark energy. The twins look at Tristan and me with wide eyes.

*"It's some kind of shield,"* Tristan says.

I push my mind out, trying to locate the source, but there's so much darkness suddenly filling the town, that nothing is distinguishable. It presses in harder, thicker. Brielle rolls her neck and shoulders. Something sparks in Elliana's eyes. The dark power is affecting them and probably not in a good way.

Shit. Shit, shit, shit.

"Girls, stay here," I order before Tristan and I rush for the door and run outside, prepared to fight whatever is out there, but the brewing storm overhead appears to have driven everyone indoors, because we find the marketplace and surrounding area vacant. Well, almost vacant. Only Camila stands in the middle of the street, alone, the wind stirring her dark hair.

"*Sheree, Aidan, and Jax, guard the twins, Dani, and Miguel!*" I yell as Tristan and I head for the town's mayor, Vanessa catching up with us.

I'm about to tell Camila to prepare for an attack, but all words and thoughts vanish when I realize Camila is not quite Camila. It's definitely the same being we'd spent the afternoon with, but not what we'd seen on the surface. And she is not at all human.

She is growing, as in physically expanding up and out, in every way. As she does, her skin darkens and mottles until it becomes an oily purplish-gray and deep black. Her limbs elongate to become proportional to her still increasing height, and they plump out with solid, defined muscle. Two horns protrude between the long locks of her black hair, growing up and curling back inward like a ram's. The whites of her eyes bleed into black, the irises and pupil glowing blood red. Fangs at least as long as my forearm protrude from under her full, black lips as she glares down at us. Unlike the Demons we've known so far, she appears to have no wings or tail, and she's clothed in a tight, black bodice that barely covers her well-endowed breasts, black pants that look painted on over perfectly proportionate curves, and black stiletto boots. Lightning flashes across the sky, momentarily illuminating her in a silvery glow. In a very strange and dark way, she's almost . . . kind of . . . *beautiful.*

If not for the deep, soul-squeezing, blackest kind of evil oozing out of her every pore and emanating across the town.

"*What the hell is that?*" Vanessa silently demands from my left as we stare up at her.

"*I'm pretty sure that's called a Major Demon,*" Tristan replies from my right.

"*I didn't think major was so literally about size.*" Neither did I. "*Are we sure it's not a Throne?*" she asks.

"No," I say. "*It's definitely a Major Demon. I've been feeling something all day, and it just occurred to me two minutes ago. I should have fucking known.*"

"You should not have rejected my offer, Alexis," the she-demon says, as she still continues to grow.

The creature that had once been Camila towers over us, nearly two stories tall … no, three stories now, her head almost even with the top of the town hall building, her horns higher than the roofline.

My wings snap out, as do Tristan's.

"Did you really think I didn't know, Shamara?" I ask as I draw my swords from their sheaths on my back, previously cloaked with my wings.

A dark purple fog appears from nowhere, surrounding us as it rolls down the streets and between the buildings, and it rises in thick curls to block anyone from seeing us. I might have misunderstood Owen's meaning. *We* are trapped—as in Tristan, Vanessa, and me, standing in the only clear area with Shamara across from us.

"I really don't want to fight you, Alexis," Shamara says, her voice deep and booming yet somehow feminine and sultry, like a giant seductress. I hardly believe her words.

"Let me guess," I reply. "You only want my daughters, and everyone else will be okay."

Her massive head tilts side to side, the horns scraping against the side of a building, knocking debris to the ground. "Hmm…something like that."

"You know that's absolutely not going to happen," Tristan says. "That's why you've done all of this—set us up like this."

"Oh, but I think it will. You just need a little convincing that you can't defeat me."

"I'm pretty sure we can," I say, spreading my wings and allowing an electric current to dance down my arms and hands, over my weapons.

"Why? Because somebody gave you the idea that it's your time to rule?" She mocks my voice with what I'd said earlier, then bends down to look at me more closely. "Don't you want to know the truth about what that means? Don't you want to know how your precious *Angels*—" she practically spits the word, her rancid breath blowing in my face— "deceived you for their own benefit? How their self-righteousness has led to this moment right now when your daughters will be turned over to me, Shamara, the greatest Major Demon to exist and the one who will open all the gates to the Thrones?"

"This is not the Angels' doing!"

"But isn't it? Are they here to deny it?" The she-demon eyes me for a moment, but I don't answer. Can't answer—because she's right about that. The Angels have abandoned me. "They've been manipulating you, Alexis. They've been manipulating the Amadis matriarchs since the beginning.

Do as they want—believe in what they want you to believe—and they will reward you very well, right? But only if you fight for them in a war you don't even understand."

"I'm pretty sure I understand the difference between good and evil."

"But do you? Don't we all believe we're on the good side? That the enemies are the *evil* ones? Are neither right? Or are both? We're all heroes in our own stories, aren't we, Alexis? You're the author—you should know." She straightens and looks down her wide nose at us, purplish black smoke curling out of her mouth as she continues. "Your Angels certainly thought they were so *good* when they denied themselves free will —by choice, which is ironic in itself. They thought that was the *benevolent* thing to do, to deny themselves the luxury of choice. Such martyrs they are. It's only turned them into resentful, manipulative, controlling beasts, no different than the rest of us. They could have chosen free will for themselves, like the fallen did, like we all did. Instead, they envy all of us who have it, including the humans. Including *you*. And now here we are, with two creatures—three, if I'm being honest, but we may let Dorian slide—who should not exist at all. But they do, because of the Angels, and now all will suffer the consequences."

I shake my head. I don't care how much truth rings in the Demon's words. I won't stand for this. "You will *not* win, Shamara. You will not have them. And you will leave the humans alone!"

The fog clears as suddenly as it had come in, and I notice people have gathered in the street.

"It's a little late for that," she says, following with a ring of laughter.

I sense the incoming evil, closer than I'd realized just moments ago, as though a blanket had been stifling it before and is now lifted, revealing it all in its full force. So much dark energy flowing all around us, and beyond the walls, too. I also sense more of my people, including Owen, sprinting for us.

"We didn't come alone," I warn.

"And I have my own army." She lifts her chin, sweeping her gaze over the growing crowd.

I glance back over my shoulder, and horror sinks like a boulder in my gut. I spin, taking it all in. So many black eyes—so many possessed humans.

"Half of this town is possessed by my followers."

A series of screams rents through the air, and people start running and shouting at each other. Complete chaos suddenly breaks out. Two black-eyed norms charge at Tristan, and he easily swats them away, but the real horror is the possessed humans attacking their own—their neighbors, their families and friends. They move swiftly, and I'm reminded of the Daemoni's attacks when they first came out to the humans, creating carnage around the world.

"Make it stop!" I yell, whirling back toward the she-demon, my swords lifted and ready.

"Hand the girls over, and I will," Shamara answers.

"Never!" I launch into the air, my wings spreading wide and lifting me to her level. "I rule here, bitch! And you will not hurt my daughters or a single other human!"

She throws her head back, more bricks flying and glass shattering, and laughs—freaking *laughs*. "The Age of Angels, you said, right? What do you think *my* kind are, Alexis? You know the stories, the origin of the Demons. Do you know the beginning of the fae, too?" She watches me for a beat and must see that I do not know, because I hang there stupidly. "Think about who the *true* Angels are—and not their mixed blood offspring." She spits those last words as she jabs a monstrous finger at me. "*You* are only an infant compared to the rest of us. So call it the Age of Angels all you want, child, but it doesn't mean what you think it does."

I blink, trying to process her words. *No. She's fucking with me. That's all. That can't be—*

I can't let her get to me. It doesn't matter what Mom and Rina had meant decades ago when they'd told me that. All that matters is the right here and right now, where my daughters and a whole town of humans will die if I don't act. More Demons are coming. I turn in the air toward the walls. They're not alone, either. Daemoni and dark fae are closing in, too.

This really has been a trap, a set-up all along. She'd stalled us, practically begging us to stay overnight, all so the others could arrive before we left. But why? What are they going to do—fight each other over my daughters? How many human lives will be lost because of it?

Not a single damn one, if I can help it.

"You cannot have them!" I shout, and I shoot a bolt of electricity at Shamara at the same time Tristan blasts her with his killing power, the one he reserves for only the direst of situations. But, of course, it doesn't even affect her.

She swings her fist at me, the gnarly claw as large as a car coming within inches of my face before I soar out of reach. Fighting escalates on the ground, my people trying to stop the possessed from attacking the remaining norms.

"*It's time*," Tristan says.

As I swing my sword at Shamara's head, it ricochets off her horn, and I know he is right. I don't need his ability to see the best solution, to come to the same conclusion that there's only one way to defeat her and end the savagery among the humans. I accept the Amadis power he's giving me, and when she feels my pull, Vanessa eagerly shares hers, too, finally getting what she's always wanted—to see my true power and shut this shit down, as she would say. I draw on the Amadis power of all of my people who are here, building it within myself and then go even beyond. It's a connection only Tristan and the other Earth's Angels know about—my ability to feed on their power, no matter where in the world they are or what they're doing, to boost my own. It's not a power I take lightly and have never used it before.

The force is enormous as it strengthens within me, filling and expanding every cell, until it presses against my skin, my bones, my organs. Until I feel like I can no longer contain it. And just as I'm about to unleash it, I feel one more powerful boost with a strength like none of the others, and I don't know where it comes from. The Angels—it has to be them, too potent to be from anyone in this world—and I'm grateful to know they haven't abandoned us after all.

"Boom," I whisper, and the energy explodes from me in a blinding white light.

The power is like a light bomb, blasting through the town, blowing out windows and making buildings tremor and the ground quake. Black smoke rises from the people—the Demonic forces—but it doesn't go back to Hell. It completely disintegrates. *Holy shit.* I didn't know I could do *that.* I know beyond a shadow of a doubt that I've ended the Demon spirits for good.

Except Shamara.

"And so it begins," the Demon says, and unlike her annihilated lessers, she explodes into a thousand black birds that swarm upward, vanishing into the stormy night sky.

There's a pause as though everyone takes a deep breath ... then more screams, louder than even before, pierce the air.

I swing around in horror and watch as the bodies begin to drop. One after another, hundreds of them. People who'd been possessed, and now, with no Demon force to keep them alive, they're gone. Every. Single. One.

A particular scream catches my attention, coming from where the girls are, and when I realize who it is—and why—I want to scream myself. No! No, no, no!

I drop to the ground and run toward them, my heart breaking, the screaming sob shattering it.

Dani falls to the floor with Miguel's lifeless body in her arms.

She lifts her dark, tear-filled eyes to me, pleading, and when I give a small shake of my head—there's nothing I can do, nothing I could have done before—something changes in her pupils, like a switch has been flipped.

When I look up, I see the same accusatory look in every other Norman's eyes:

I killed their loved ones.

omplete numbness overcomes me as I watch the bodies piling up and hear Dani's cries and Elliana's whispers as she tries to console her. My breath feels frozen in my lungs, my heart as though it's stopped beating. I feel like I'm caught in another dimension, unable to respond, to move, to even feel, only to see and hear. Then one feeling settles in: complete and utter horror.

What have I done?

A deep voice bellows in my mind. "*Get the twins the fuck out of there! More are coming!*"

Dorian's shout slams me back into the moment, my heart jumping against my chest.

"It's not over," Owen says a moment later, finally joining us. "We have to get out of here. *Now.*"

I lunge for Brielle, and Vanessa grabs Elliana, trying to pull her away from Dani.

"No!" Elliana screams. "I'm staying!"

"The hell you are," Tristan growls.

"The hell I'm leaving Dani," she snaps back.

I jerk my chin at Vanessa, who wraps her arms around Elli, hauling her out the door. Elli kicks and throws her head back, smashing Vanessa's nose hard enough I can hear the bone crack. The vampire growls, and if it had been anyone besides her niece, they'd probably be dead by now.

"*Owen, bound Elliana before she really harms someone,*" I order, and he throws a spell around my daughter. Her arms press into her sides, and her legs can only move enough to walk.

"Asshole," Elliana grits out, still bucking against the magical hold, but at least she can't hurt him. "I need to get back to Dani!"

Sheree, Aidan, Jax, and the guards fall in around the twins, and they quickly escort them down the street, Elliana cussing them out the whole way. Tristan and I take to the air just above them, scouting for a quiet, dark corner where we can pause long enough for Owen to create a portal, but the chaos is everywhere. Norms pour into the streets with guns aimed at us. We swat away the bullets, but they keep shooting anyway. Nowhere is safe. Beyond the gates, just as Dorian had warned, more Demons, as well as Daemoni and fae, gather.

"*What do we do?*" I ask Tristan, trying not to let panic overwhelm me.

"*Go north.*" Dorian pushes a visual into my mind of a clear area beyond the town's north gate. I silently tell Owen to change course and head that way. Fat raindrops begin to fall as the group on the ground winds through the pathways created by the hodgepodge of structures that fill Misery's Edge.

Realizing they're wasting precious ammunition, the armed norms abandon their mission to shoot us down, but Demons fly toward us now. Tristan and I soar at them, heading them off before they reach the twins. More surround us, and as we fight them, I lose sight of our people, but I can still sense their minds as they flee for safety. So far, so good. But I know that won't last long. We need a complete escape, or this will be never-ending.

"*Find Dorian,*" I tell Tristan once we've slashed through the throng of Demons and have a free moment. I soar for the twins to ensure they're okay, my heart racing and unable to calm until I see they're not harmed.

Owen begins to open a portal when Tristan drops to the ground, Dorian right next to him. Everyone gasps at the sight of my son.

"I'm here to help, but we have to make it fast." He eyes his sisters for a moment before turning his attention on me, and I can't help it. I rush over to him and throw my arms around his neck. His dark energy zaps through me, and I notice how similar it is to the girls'. I want to believe that it's a good thing—that he's changing for the better—but I fear it's the other way around—the girls are not. "My offer still stands," he murmurs.

I step away and look at Tristan then back to Dorian, always amazed at how similar yet how different they look to each other. "Can we still use it? Can they still go?"

"The gate's still open, yes. The rest is up to you."

Blowing out a breath, I turn toward Tristan, silently pleading for another option, but already knowing his answer.

"I don't see any better solutions, Lex," he says

I swallow the lump in my throat that just might be my heart and nod. "Okay. We have to keep them safe."

Dorian gives Owen the coordinates, and the warlock swiftly opens a portal. I send all of the guards with Aidan to head back to The Loft and ensure our people there are safe. The rest of us rush through the portal to a black pebbled beach bordering a churning sea under a twilight sky, our breaths hanging visibly in the freezing air. I sense the gate before I see it, nothing more than what appears to be a mirage hanging in the air, not all that different from Owen's portals. Very much different than the girls' gate, surrounded by the forest of metal-like vines and trees. The energy emitting from it is just as much of a contrast, feeling lighter and welcoming.

Brielle stares at it a moment before looking at me then her father with questions in her eyes. Elli just glares at the ground, her nostrils flaring as she stews in her anger.

"The world beyond is another Earth," Tristan explains. "A version like ours in an alternate universe, but it's also very different. It's a good place. You'll see."

"You've been there?" Brielle asks.

He nods, barely glancing at me, and I wonder if he's about to tell them everything—what we'd started just … yesterday? Two days ago? It feels like years. Right here and right now are probably not the best time or place.

"Your mom and I went a couple of years ago to check it out," he says. "We'd considered it as an option to keep you safe."

"We thought—" I begin, but I correct myself. "*I* thought we could keep you safe here. I don't know that we can any longer." The admission comes out quietly, and I hate that we've been driven to this point. But I'll do whatever it takes now to protect them, even if it means saying goodbye. Even if it means being worlds away, quite literally.

"Wait." Elliana finally lifts her gaze, looking directly at me. "You can't be serious! We're not going there, are we? To another *world*?"

"We all are," Tristan replies, and Elli's eyes grow wide with horror, her head shaking violently. Before she can say anything, he continues, his voice leaving no room for argument, although she'll probably try anyway. "In case you didn't notice, Elliana, war is imminent, and your and Brielle's lives are at the center of it all. Hundreds of souls were just obliterated to protect you. Do not make their deaths in vain. Do not make *Miguel's* death pointless."

She scowls at this, but he knew exactly where to drive the point home because she doesn't argue anymore as we hastily make plans. While we discuss, Dorian reaches into his suit coat's inner pocket and pulls a large wad of hundred-dollar bills from the Before time and hands it to me.

"I found it not too long ago. It's useless here, but if that world's money is the same, you'll need it. It can at least get you started."

I take the money with a heart full of gratitude—not just for the cash but for my son. I've believed all along that there's still hope for his soul, and I'm so glad I was right, not for my sake, but his.

"Sheree and Jax, stay here with Dorian," I say. "Protect the gate while we go through. Owen and Vanessa, you're coming with us."

Vanessa doesn't even try to hide her excitement, her mouth stretching into a beam.

"I'll cloak it when we return," Owen tells Dorian. "We have to ensure nobody else can find it."

Tristan leads them all toward the gate, but I turn to my son. "Thank you, Dorian. For everything."

He nods, his eyes filled with an unfathomable swirl of conflict. "Until the end, Mom."

I give a half-smile over my shoulder as I stride over to the others. "Until the end."

As we're about to go through the gate, Sasha suddenly drops in next to us. I wonder where she's been, but not for long. Black Demon blood stains her muzzle. She'd been fighting to protect the girls, too.

"Sasha," Dorian says with a boyish grin. The *lykora* nudges his hand with her snout before shrinking into a small dog. "Protect them."

Although she answers to the girls now, she gives a dip of her head before leaping into Brielle's arms.

A moment later, following Tristan, the girls, and Vanessa, I step off the rocky beach and onto a snow-covered clearing on the side of a mountain, Owen right behind me. While he closes the portal, I gaze far below to the picturesque small town cradled in a box canyon like something off a Christmas card in the Before time—which is the Now time here.

It's so pristine and peaceful here, it really is a whole different world.

The peace is interrupted when the twins both gasp and then their wings suddenly burst out of their backs. My muscles tense as I wonder what they're about to do—like take off in flight—but then they both fall to the ground, laughing hysterically. Vanessa looks over at me with a raised brow. I can only shake my head.

"An adverse reaction to the dimension?" I ask.

Tristan rubs his jaw, his eyes contemplative, but there's a touch of humor in his voice when he says, "Feel for it, Lex. Feel their energy."

I send my senses out, and I gasp out loud, too. I haven't realized how weighed down they'd been with that dark energy until now—when it's gone. Completely vanished, as if it never existed. They feel so … *light*. Almost like they're the embodiment of Amadis power. And speaking of power—

"*The spell's been broken,*" I say to Tristan, and he nods. "*Well, that complicates things.*"

He nods again. If their memories come back now, of all times, we could have serious problems.

Movement not too far down the mountain catches our attention, and I know we can't discuss it now. We won't be alone much longer.

"Get the girls to Denver," Tristan tells Owen as I give some money to Vanessa. "Alexis and I will handle the leaders here and hopefully negotiate a deal."

We know from past experience how protective they are of their little town, and for good reason. Fortunately, they respect the Angels—they appreciate their power, including ours. We just have to hope it's enough to convince them to agree to a huge favor.

It takes hours, but we finally negotiate a hearing in a few days for them to consider our proposal. By the time Tristan and I get to Denver and track down the girls, Owen, and Vanessa, they're settled in at a small hotel. I'm surprised to find Brielle and Elliana sound asleep. I'd expected them to be hyped up on their own power combined with the complete culture shock of the city. Owen explains it's been more like an overload shock to their system, because they crashed hard. Of course, I'm sure it helps that they're snuggled into clean, comfortable beds like nothing they've ever experienced in our world.

Tristan and I should probably grab a couple of hours of regeneration, too, but I know I can't possibly sleep. Not here, in this place that's so much like how our world had been before the war yet feels so alien. And not only because it's more technologically advanced than we'd been twenty years ago. More because I'm not the same. None of us are.

How can I even consider leaving my daughters here in this strange world?

A blaring sound jolts me out of sleep.

I shoot up and spring to my feet, my heart slamming against my chest and my palms out, ready to blast my power. Disoriented, I look around the dark room, the only light coming from the television screen. The blaring sound a siren outside in the city streets, already fading in the distance. No Shamara, no Demons, not even Daemoni. Just the sounds of humanity in the city. What had once been a part of our normal everyday life feels so foreign.

"We're safe here," I whisper out loud as I breathe the way Chandra has taught me to calm my heart. Whatever I'd been dreaming has already vanished from my mind, but I have no doubt it was about home. Fear and guilt for what we left behind—for what I've done—have been tearing me apart, battling with the need to protect my daughters. "The girls are safe. They'll be okay."

"If you don't count the detriments of too much screen time," Tristan murmurs, taking my hand and pulling me back down into the bed, into his arms. "They woke up hours ago and have been enthralled with the T.V. all night. Still."

I don't remember drifting off, but I'd apparently been wrong about not being able to sleep here. I suppose being awake for a few days straight will do that. Peering at the digital clock, I see it's near dawn on our second full day in this world.

"They take after their father," I say, snuggling into his chest. "Always so fascinated with his toys."

He chuckles. "And guess what we'll be doing today? They'll need some toys to live here. Chronologically, this world is behind ours by a few years, but its technology has advanced exponentially. They'll need laptops, tablets, and phones, to start with."

"To start with," I murmur. "And how do you plan to purchase those? I'm pretty sure between the hotel, food, and the shopping trip for normal clothes yesterday has wiped out what Dorian gave us."

Thank the Angels the currency looks the same here. It felt a little like using counterfeit money, but we didn't have much choice. We can't run around this world in our fighting leathers. I'd been a little concerned taking the girls out at all. Not just because everything is so strange to them here, but also because I don't know what to expect now that the spell on their powers has been broken. But so far, they seem better than ever, like they left all of that dark energy in our world. Which will help in convincing the leaders of that small town in the mountains to let them stay.

"While you four were shopping yesterday, Owen and I went to a couple of the caves Chandra had shown us in our world to collect gemstones. They're still untouched here, so we gathered some rocks, sold them, and I've already put half of the money in the markets."

"Of course, you have," I say with a snort. He'd always been good at the markets, needing only basic facts to select the best trades. That had been one of his jobs when I first met him.

"The girls will be set while they're here."

The news brings relief, but also a little discomfort. "It kind of feels like stealing."

"We harvested the gems naturally. Well, naturally with magic. Nobody knew the clusters were even there, and we're putting the money back into their own economy. It's no different than someone from this world finding the caves and mining it."

"I suppose. As long as we don't take anything back with us. What belongs in this world stays here." I also make a mental note to ensure we —or at least the girls, since they'll be here longer—do some charity work to give back to this place that is basically saving their lives.

As long as they'll be able to stay.

Tristan, Owen, and I return to the small town the next day for our hearing with the leaders. Thankfully, we're able to negotiate a deal—the timing for them couldn't have been any better. They'll even reinforce the memory spell, which they're apparently very good at. The arrangement stirs up all kinds of conflicting emotions for me, but I try to focus on the gift that the whole situation is providing.

"You're going to college!" I tell the girls when Tristan and I return, my excitement a little exaggerated because I know we'll have to sell the idea to them. We've already sent Owen and Vanessa on a mission to help it all go smoother. I hope. "It's a special school for supernaturals," I continue even as they gape at me, "but it's still college. You'll have all the experiences of dorms and parties and classes and everything. And you'll learn—"

"This is fucking ridiculous," Elliana says, cutting me off.

"Watch your mouth, Elli," I remind her, but she rolls her eyes.

"I learned it from you."

I sigh. I can't argue with that, but I give her the Mom look anyway before replying. "It's not ridiculous. It's an opportunity. A miracle even. It will be fun!"

I can hear the inauthenticity in my own voice and cringe.

"Are you *kidding* me?" Elli shouts.

"You didn't really think we'd get excited about being left here, did you?" Brielle chimes in. "After what we just left behind? And all because of us. You can't expect us to stay here in this unreal world when all of you will be fighting a war."

My excitement immediately deflates at the reminder. As if I need reminding. The thought of what we left behind, what we'll be going back to has been niggling at the back of my mind nonstop, digging a hole in my gut that grows deeper and deeper with each passing hour we're here.

"We're hoping it won't come to another war," Tristan says, taking my hand and giving it a squeeze. "And if we know you two are safe here, your mom and I can focus on preventing such a war."

Elliana drops her hands to her hips and simply glares at me. I know why. I know the pain she's feeling over Dani and Miguel. And she can't possibly know the fear I harbor for her life.

"We should be there helping you," Brielle insists. "If you can't prevent it, we can fight."

Tristan's eyes spark. "The hell you will."

"You've taught us—"

Elli cuts her off. "Forget it, Brie. We're not going to change their minds. Besides, they're right. We're better off here." My brows pull together, wondering where this sudden change of heart comes from. Then she finishes, "And our world is better without us there."

"Oh, Elli, that's not true," I say, squeezing her arm.

She twists away, jerking her arm free. "Of course, it is. None of this would have happened, if not for us."

My heart sinks. I want them to understand the danger they're in and what others are doing to protect them, but I haven't considered how much guilt they would take on for what I had done. I'm grateful we've decided not to tell them the rest of the story—the truth about their disappearance and their return. Before coming back here to the hotel to deliver the news of the hearing's outcome, Tristan and I had discussed if we should decline the offer regarding the memory spell and disclose everything to the twins. On the one hand, they deserve to know. On the other, how could we dump it in their laps right before leaving them in a strange world? I don't want the two events tied to each other. I don't want them to feel like we're abandoning them because of what they'd done. I don't want them to carry any more guilt than they already are.

"Wrong," Tristan replies. "Evil has existed for eons before the two of you ever did. You didn't open the gate on purpose, but even if you never had, evil would have found another reason to rear its ugly head. It always does. Don't blame yourselves, either one of you. You two are innocents."

"And we've defeated it before," I add. "We'll do it again. We just need to know you two are safe from those who are after you—those who want to use you or kill you. We won't allow either to happen." A lump forms in my throat, and I blink away the pricks at the back of my eyes. "I will *not* lose another child to them."

Brielle moves closer and slides an arm over my shoulders. "Do you really think leaving us here is the answer, though, Mom?"

Tristan answers for me. "It's the best solution. Removing you two from the picture and making you completely inaccessible changes everything. Our enemies will need a whole new strategy, and while they're regrouping, we can work on our allies to prevent another war from breaking out."

"Then we can go back?" Elliana asks, her voice full of hope.

# CHAPTER 11

*I* nod in answer to Elliana's question, not able to elaborate any more than that. Because the truth is that I don't know how long that will be. We've negotiated a deal to allow the twins to stay in that small town and attend the new school the leaders are starting to train a supernatural army, in exchange that they will fight for that town and this world if ever necessary. Considering my daughters' whole life has been about fighting for survival, it's a pretty good deal. The town is the best place to hide them because it's so well warded from outsiders, safer than anywhere else they could be in this world. They can stay for however long they need to be here—as long as they don't bring our world's problems to this one. There are a couple of other conditions, which we'll have to explain soon enough.

"In the meantime, you get to go to college," I say, trying to infuse my words with the enthusiasm from earlier but knowing it falls flat, especially when I see the doubt in their eyes.

"You'll be able to learn a lot here," Tristan says. "Things we don't have the resources to teach anymore. Brielle, maybe you can learn how to bring technology back to our world. Elliana, you can learn how to put your need for adventure to good use. Your being here is not a waste of time. You *will* be helping us, more than you realize."

Their expressions shift, and while I don't pry into their minds to know what they're thinking—as if they'd ever let me—I can sense that this comforts them some.

"We're hoping for another benefit," I add. "The magic in this world is completely different. It comes from a great many sources, including other realms. But none of them are dark. That gate hasn't been opened here. So we're hoping that connection the darkness seems to have to you two is severed for good. You two already seem . . . I don't know . . . better here. Your energy is different. Especially yours, Elli."

Again, I don't read their minds, but I know we're all thinking about the silver utensils the girls are now able to use without any kind of reaction. Physical proof that they're different here.

The girls exchange a look, and I know they're doing that twin mind-talk thing, but it's only for a brief moment.

Then Elliana grins, though I'm not sure how authentic it is. "Yeah, you're right. I do feel better here."

"Same," Brielle chirps.

"You're right, too, Dad—I mean Tristan," Elli corrects. Because they don't look much younger than us, we're playing the old charade Mom and I used to do—that they're my sisters rather than our children. "Bringing us here really is the best solution for all. By the time you've fixed everything there, Brie and I will be good to go."

"Thanks for being upfront with us," Brielle says. "It really helped us to understand."

I return their smiles, but I'm not buying their BS. It's obvious they're saying what they think we want to hear. I don't call them out, though. I can't—our time alone with the girls is about to end.

"Excellent," Tristan says, and I know he doesn't buy it either, but he goes along with them. "We're so glad you two see it our way. And you'll be really happy to know that you won't be left here completely alone."

With a swish of his hand, the door to the suite unlocks and opens. Owen and Vanessa have returned from the mission I'd sent them on, their charge right behind them.

"Charleigh!" Elliana practically shrieks when she sees her, and she rushes for her best friend, swallowing her in a hug. "What are you doing here?"

"I'm going to college with you!" And it is her presence and excitement that we needed to convince the girls that this is a good thing for them.

"Blossom and Jax okayed it?" I ask Owen, making sure he at least asked. Although I'm the matriarch, I'm not about to take someone's child away against their will. Not that Charleigh's a child anymore.

Owen nods. "It took a bit of convincing—"

"You mean a lot of convincing," Vanessa corrects him.

Owen shrugs. "They knew she'd be safer here, too."

"And a lot less miserable," Charleigh says. "Life would have sucked without you two to keep it interesting. Besides—" She looks at me with a lifted brow. "I swore a vow to you. They are mine to protect, and I don't take that lightly."

My heart swells with pride as I study all three of them. My fear of leaving them—of being literally worlds away—remains, but not quite as strong as it had been before. I know they'll be okay here. In fact, I have a feeling they're going to thrive. True excitement for all of the fun and adventures they're going to have begins to replace the false bravado I've been putting on since we arrived. I've wanted a life like this for my daughters since the day they were born, thinking it could never come true. This really is like a miracle, an answer to a dream.

I remind myself that when the day comes we have to leave. When Owen returned to our world to retrieve Charleigh, he discovered we'd already lost a couple of weeks at home. Our people need Tristan and me. We can't stay any longer.

"So part of our deal is that we can't keep returning to check up on you," I tell the girls on our last morning with them. Vanessa is with the four of us in the hotel room while the guys pack the few things the girls have already purchased because it's time for them to leave the city, too. "It would defeat the whole purpose of trying to hide you, but we have a way to keep in touch. It might not be perfect, especially with entire dimensions between us, but it should at least enable me to feel you and know you're safe. Charleigh, I'll need your witchy assistance with this."

I pull out my dagger and remove my shirt. The girls gasp when I start digging the blade into my chest, over my heart. A few moments later, I dislodge the faerie stone. With my guidance, Charleigh magically breaks it into three pieces, imbues it with some extra protective energy, then embeds a piece into my daughters' chests and one back into mine. It already warms as soon as I feel out for them. I can only hope it works half as well once I'm home and they're . . . not.

"One other condition is that you'll need to start training before school starts in August," I tell them as we finish getting ready. "I think you'll really like your teacher. She's a witch-hybrid and super cool. She's powerful, though, even more than Charleigh. She can help you learn your powers to their fullest extent."

And I'm not wrong. Owen takes us to the mountains, where we're immediately greeted near the gate back to our world. The girls instantly take a liking to their new mentor, and I know they'll be okay here. In fact, I'm surprised at how calm I am when it comes time to say goodbye.

"If you ever need anything, use the stone," I say to Brielle as I hold her tightly against me. "And in worst case scenario, Charleigh knows the way home." And only Charleigh—she's sworn an unbreakable vow to me to not tell the girls, especially not Elliana, unless the situation is dire and they need to return home.

"We'll be okay here, Mom," Brielle whispers as she squeezes me back. "Even Elli. Charleigh and I will make sure of it."

When we release and trade with Tristan, I grasp Elliana tightly, hoping her sister is right.

"You've always wanted an adventure," I say to her. "What bigger adventure can there be than this?"

She pulls a little away to look me in the eye and nods. "I will make the most of it while I'm here. I promise, Mom. I mean, the clothes are amazing, and the food is to die for. How can we not love it? But when I come home—and we *will* come home—you better put me on your damn elite team! You know I will be the best Demon assassin who's ever lived, especially now that I have revenge on my mind."

I can't help but smile as I pull her back against me, selfishly happy that she's now considering Shamara the villain and not just me. "You will be the best at anything you do. I know it. I love you so much, Elliana." I step back to look at both of my girls, fighting the tears and swelling emotions throbbing in my chest. "I love both of you across all the worlds and all the universes, until the end of forever and always."

"Until the end," they both say, and I feel their love warming the stone in my chest as Tristan and I step through the gate.

We answer together, one more time, before the gate closes, "Until the end."

# EPILOGUE

$O$wen had told us about the time loss. He'd failed to tell us everything that happened while we'd been gone.

"I knew you'd see soon enough," he says when we return to The Loft, "but it's apparently even worse now."

We'd been in that other world for a week, but we return nearly a month later here. We don't think time actually passes faster here. Rather, Tristan surmises that crossing dimensions means crossing the full time-space continuum, so we move back and forth in time as well as space. Or something like that. He has a better grasp of it than I do. I just know that returning is almost like when the war had started and due to a tricky portal and other events, we'd been removed from civilization for several weeks and returned to a whole different world. The change isn't quite as drastic as then, but the nearly abandoned Loft, by both our people and those who'd been stalking it, tells me nothing is the same.

When Owen and Vanessa had come to retrieve Charleigh, my core team—Blossom, Jax, Sheree, Aidan, and Carlie—and some of our guards had been working to clear The Loft out, sending our people off to find new homes because it was no longer safe here. Now they're the only ones left.

"They're calling it the Massacre at the Edge, and now you're wanted by all the factions, but primarily the humans, dead or alive," Blossom tells me as we gather around a table in the dining area. No need to hide in the conference room when there's nobody else around.

"Preferably dead, though," Jax adds, quite comfortingly.

It really does feel like when the last war began and Tristan and I had topped the most-wanted lists. This time, though, it's warranted. Although nobody would understand that the humans who died in Misery's Edge that night were no longer themselves, I still had essentially killed them. And hundreds of people had witnessed it.

Tristan folds his hands on the table. "We need to find allies. The light fae are our best bet."

"So we'll need to see if we can reach Bree," I say.

"We haven't heard from her in two years," he reminds me. "It might be easier to find Jessica or Lisa, or even Stacey or Debbie."

"We haven't seen any of them for longer than two years," Sheree points out.

"Your mother always seems to arrive precisely when we need her," I say. "Bree came to warn us about the girls right after they came home. Maybe she's been waiting for this moment."

"If she doesn't?" Aidan asks. "Can't you just go to Faery yourself, Tristan?"

"I don't know where the portals are," he says.

"Ah, well, I do," the gargoyle replies. We all gape at him. This is the first time he's ever mentioned this. He shrugs. "It's in Scotland, but I can take you."

Sheree places a hand on his arm. "That sounds . . . like a dangerous journey."

He shrugs again. "There are other portals, but I don't know where."

"Dorian probably does," Tristan says, rubbing the back of his neck. "He goes to Faery often."

"Really?" I ask, my brow furrowing. Our son has mentioned Faery to me before, but I didn't realize he spent much time there. "Do you think he'll help again?"

"Of course, he will!" Blossom says, but everyone else looks skeptical. She'd been the only one not surprised that he'd helped us with the twins, her faith in him never wavering, maybe even stronger than my own.

"I don't know," Aidan says. "From what we've heard, the Daemoni and the Demons don't know what he did for ya, and it almost seems like he's tryin' to prove that he's still with them."

Not understanding, I look at Sheree, wondering if she knows. She frowns.

"Word is that Dorian is still very much in charge of the Daemoni and leading them on raids of norm towns. It's also been said he's quite friendly with the dark fae, the Unseelie king, more specifically."

"The what?" I ask, confused.

"The Unseelie fae rule the dark fae. Obviously, the king rules them all," Blossom says. "Robin brought us that most recent report a few days ago. The fae are all over this. They really want your daughters and will go right through you to get them."

"Well, they're safe. Thanks to their brother." I look at Tristan. "Do you think he's still playing both sides?"

His hazel gaze holds mine as he considers the possible answers. "Dorian's more powerful than any of them. He holds the cards. To be honest, I can't say for certain what he's doing, except that he's playing his own game."

"Which makes him dangerous," Aidan says, always suspicious of everyone. Of course, out of everybody here, he's the only one who didn't know Dorian as a child, before he went to the Daemoni.

More discussion ensues about whether to trust Dorian, and other ideas are thrown out about how to find Faery, but Dorian seems to be our only answer. I think we can trust him, and I'm about to say so, when we all freeze, listening.

"*Someone's here,*" I say to everyone, and they all nod, sensing it, too. "*I can't find a mind signature, though.*"

"Alexis?" the familiar squeaky voice calls from the tunnel that leads to the surface. Then I realize why I hadn't sensed her mind—she's fae.

We all flash to her, finding the green-haired pixie who'd poisoned me so many years ago. She'd become an ally since, but we haven't seen her in over a decade. And she's not alone.

"How did you get in?" I demand, eyeing the two fae with her—one with purple and white hair, the other with pink and white. Although they're even shorter than me, they seem to tower over the pixie.

"I guess the wards still allow me," the pixie says with a small shrug. "These two heard their names through the veil and were trying to find you. They say they can help."

I peer at Stacey and Debbie, the two fae who used to reside in England when they were in this world. The two who had kept Tristan and me alive right after the bombs dropped. I hadn't seen them since releasing them from Hell, though.

"We need Bree," Tristan says, crossing his arms over his chest.

"Bree won't come," Stacey, the pink-haired one, replies, still with that English accent, which doesn't really make sense for a faerie. "She's with the royal court now, busy, busy, busy."

"Can you take us to her?" I ask.

Debbie's bright blue eyes widen as she shakes her head. "Oh, no. We do not have that authority."

"But we can tell you how to find the portal," Stacey says, lifting her white brows.

"For what cost?" Owen asks.

Debbie bats her eyelashes at him. "Oh, love, I can think of a few things you can do for me."

Vanessa growls, and all three fae jump back.

"Just tell us where the portal is," I say. We'll pay whatever they want us to pay. Well, not with Owen, but I'm sure they'll take other payment.

"Just you two," Stacey says, shaking a finger at Tristan and me. "He's part-faerie, so he'll get you in. But the Seelie queen will likely only meet with you, Alexis."

"Seelie is ruled by a queen?" I ask, surprised.

"Yes," Stacey answers.

"No," Debbie says at the same time, and they glare at each other for a moment. "The king rules."

"Psh." Stacey waves a hand in the air. "If you want anything done, you need to speak with the queen. The king only wants war with the Unseelie king. He cares nothing about anything else."

So we make plans to meet the queen. Or, at least, to find Bree in Faery so she can help us get an audience with the queen. Blossom, Jax, Sheree, and Aidan will take Carlie to Amadis Island, where Noah, my uncle, has been gathering the Earth's Angels and Amadis. Vanessa and Owen will go as far as they can with Tristan and me, then return to the rest.

But as soon as we flash to the redwood forest in the Pacific Northwest, near the site of the portal to Faery, we're ambushed. The moment I appear, I have long enough to take in the huge tree trunks before something slams into my head and everything goes black.

I don't know how long I'm out or where I am when I wake, but it's not in the redwood forest. It's cold here—a chill I feel in my very bones. It's a dark room . . . wait. I blink, and flickering light dances in my vision.

Fire? Yes, it looks like flames skitter along the surface in front of me, a surface of shiny black stone, perhaps onyx or obsidian. It takes me a moment to realize I'm not seeing actual flames, but the reflections of fire on a polished stone floor.

I'm on my hands and knees. My whole body hurts as though I've been beaten, but that doesn't make sense. My body regenerates too quickly for this kind of pain. I also feel some kind of magical restraint pressing in on me, preventing my wings from showing, suppressing my powers.

Lifting my head, I blink as I try to look around. It takes me a moment to orient myself. Tristan is next to me, also on his knees, but I sense him more than see him. I also sense several bodies around us, towering over us. Evil—every single one of them oozes horribly evil energy. Demons? The Ancients? I'm not sure.

Squinting my eyes, I peer at the shape before us, forcing my eyes and my mind to focus. I gasp when the vision clears to a very handsome man dressed all in black sprawled on a throne made of the same stone as the floor and the walls.

"Dorian?" I whisper.

"Hello, Mother, Father," he says, almost drawling the words as though he's bored.

"What are you doing, son?" Tristan growls, his voice rougher than I've ever heard it before.

Dorian tilts his head and spreads his hands. "I'm doing exactly what needs to be done. Thank you for making it all so easy, by the way. Every step of the way, from getting my sisters right where I need them to flashing straight into my trap, you've been so cooperative. I sincerely appreciate it. Now, where should we start?"

He stares at us for a moment, as though seriously expecting us to answer, although the question seems rhetorical. I can't form a single coherent thought, my mind swirling with images, from him helping us with the twins to the girls left in a strange world by themselves—only Dorian able to get to them. Shit. Fuck. Damn.

Dorian leans forward, his mouth stretching into a frightening grin and his eyes filling with a red glow. "How about we start with this: your little Age of Angels has come to an end, Mother. Your time to rule is over. It's *my* time now."

What happens next? Read Knights of Souls and Shadows, Book 1 .

*Word of mouth is very important for any author. If you enjoyed the book, please consider leaving a review, even if it's only a sentence or two. This is one of the most important and appreciated things you can do for an author.*

# GLOSSARY & CAST

*A reminder of who and what you've discovered so far in the Soul Savers world.*

**Aidan** - Gargoyle shifter from Scotland.

**A.K. Emerson** – Alexis's famous pen name.

**Alexis Ames Knight** – Amadis matriarch. Married to Tristan Knight and mother of Dorian. Youngest daughter to ever go through the Ang'dora and to become matriarch. Her bio father is the leader of the Daemoni. Known abilities include telepathy, electricity, telekinesis, super strength, speed and senses, Amadis power.

**Alys** – Recently converted Amadis vampire.

**Amadis** (uh-MAH-dees) – Secret matriarchal society that serves as the Angels' army on Earth, currently led by Alexis Ames Knight. Their purpose is to defend human souls from the Daemoni and to convert Daemoni souls to Amadis. Consist of a variety of supernatural beings.

**Amadis daughters** – Women of the bloodline of the original creator of the Amadis. Each daughter eventually serves as the matriarch.

**Amadis power** – A special power of love and light gifted to the Amadis by the Angels. The Amadis daughters receive it during the Ang'dora. Other society members are granted a lower level of power upon conversion and official acceptance into the Amadis.

**Ammi** – Started the London cell of AK's Angels with her sister Kristen. Turned into a vampire and converted immediately by Char and Alexis.

**Andrew** – The Angel who fell from Heaven and fathered Cassandra and Jordan before eventually ascending (read about it in *Genesis: A Soul Savers Novella*).

**Ang'dora** – Literally means "gift of the Angels" (Ang = angels, dora = Greek word for gifts). An enigmatic change all Amadis daughters go through to receive their powers and supernatural abilities. Usually happens in middle age, after the daughter has experienced major milestones of life as a human, but Alexis went through it quite early. Except for Sophia, no Amadis daughter has given birth after the Ang'dora.

**Angels** – Spirits of Heaven who (primarily) remain in the Otherworld. Most fight in the age-old war with Demons, battling for human souls.

**Armand** – French vampire on Rina's council, he oversees Amadis police force and is anti-Tristan. Killed by Daemoni.

**Attair** – Amadis warlock from Arabia who's on Rina's council and is anti-Tristan.

**Baby Cakes** – Faerie who's a friend of Bree, so she's helped Tristan and Alexis. For a price, surely.

**Blossom** – Alexis's best friend and council member. Amadis witch from the Daytona coven.

**Bree** – Tristan's birth mother. Fae.

**Brielle Sophia Ames Knight** – Baby daughter of Alexis and Tristan, twin to Elliana, sister to Dorian. Currently an unknown creature with wings.

**Brogan** – Amadis vampire, turned when the Daemoni first came out to the humans during the war. After retiring from the military, he started The Prepper's Stash House, a multi-million dollar doomsday prep company, which turned out to be a really good thing for Alexis and A.K.'s Angels, who converted him to Amadis. He's much cooler than his nephew, James.

**Cam** - A summoned son, now an Earth's Angel

**Carlie** – Alexis's human classmate during her first year at college. Now a doctor in D.C.

**Cassandra** – Half angel, half human who started the Amadis (read her story in *Genesis: A Soul Savers Novella*).

**Chandra** – Amadis were-leopard and member of the matriarch's council who oversees the region of India.

**Charlotte Allbright** – Amadis warlock, Owen's mother, Sophia's best friend, and overall badass aunt figure to Alexis.

**Cloak** – A magic spell performed by mages that hides or makes invisible its subject. Often used in conjunction with a shield.

**Conversion** – The process of eliminating dark or light energy and replacing it with the opposite, then indoctrinating the supernatural being into the new society. The Amadis purpose is to convert Daemoni souls before they become damned, destroyed, or forever lost. However, on occasion, Amadis members will convert to the Daemoni (e.g., Ian).

**Cruz** – A Daemoni were-jaguar.

**Daemoni** (day-MAH-nee) – Satan's servants as the Demons' army on Earth, currently led by Lucas. They turn humans to harvest their souls and build their army. The Amadis try to stop them.

**Daniela (Dani)** - A norm with abilities, and Elliana's first "love."

**Debbie** – Faerie in England who helps Alexis and Tristan from time to time. Cohorts with Stacey, another faerie.

**Demons** – Spirits from Hell, some being angels that fell from Heaven with Satan as his followers and others being his creations. They take various physical forms, including horned and winged beasts and possessors of human meat suits.

**Dorian Knight** – Son of Alexis and Tristan, unknown creature but currently human. Known abilities include self-healing and flying. Converting to Daemoni?

**Dragons** - One of the many creatures that had disappeared from this realm when they were captured by Satan and held prisoners in Hell

**Earth's Angels** – Newly created by the Angels, on the lowest rung of the Angel hierarchy, includes Alexis, Tristan, the Summoned sons who have converted back to Amadis, as well as their offspring. Alexis leads them.

**Edmund** – Summoned son and member of the Daemoni. Known abilities include flashing, super strength and speed, idiocy, and being an overall douche-canoe.

**Elliana Katerina Ames Knight** – Baby daughter of Alexis and Tristan, twin to Brielle, sister to Dorian. Currently an unknown creature with wings.

**Ethan** - Leader of the dragon clan closest to The Loft

**Eris** – Daemoni witch from ancient times who helped Jordan create the potion that changed everything (read about it in *Genesis: A Soul Savers Novella*).

**Faeries/Fae** – Little is known about the fae as they tend to stay away from human affairs, as well as those of the Amadis and Daemoni. A handful do enjoy wreaking havoc in the Earthly realm, and sometimes they may even help out. They're considered Otherworldly creatures, because their world is not exactly part of Earth. They closely guard their secrets about the Faerie realm.

**Ferrer** – Blacksmith mage who lives on Amadis Island.

**Fertility Stone** – The faerie stone Bree gave Tristan when he was a young boy, embedding it in his heart with the instructions to give it to his true mate. Only when she has possession of it can he father children. The stone also allows the holder to share their emotions so he could feel his mate's love—but also the possessor's darker emotions.

**Flashing** – The supernatural ability to transport to another location up to a hundred miles away (give or take) in the blink of an eye. While objects can be held or attached to the body during a flash, Tristan is the only known creature who can flash while carrying another person. While both Daemoni and Amadis can flash, it's not necessarily a natural ability for all—some creatures have to be assisted by mages.

**Galina** – Russian Amadis warlock and a member of the matriarch's council, she favors Tristan and Alexis.

**Gargoyles** - Little is known about them, as Aidan is the first to be seen in many centuries. They're somehow connected to the dragons.

**Hades** – Daemoni HQ, an underground city in the Taymyr Peninsula of Siberia.

**Heather** – Human girl, Dorian's babysitter and friend, daughter of Phil and sister to Sonya.

**Hellfire** – Direct from Hell, used by Demons, one of the few things that can scar, severely maim, and possibly kill Alexis and Tristan.

**Hunters** – Humans (or are they?) who know about the supernatural creatures and kill them.

**Ian** – Member of the Daemoni, converted from the Amadis. Known abilities include compensating for his minuscule junk by spilling secrets, causing problems with the Amadis, and ruining Alexis's life.

**James** – The boy Alexis punched in the nose when she was a teenager. Later became a hunter, and they met up again in D.C.

**Jaxon** – Were-croc from the Australian Outback who's become part of Alexis's team. Blossom's beau.

**Jeana** – Sorceress who tortured Alexis and Owen to learn Lucas and Kali's secret about the Norman soldiers. Mate of Merrick. Dead.

**Jelani** – Wizard from Africa who is one of the matriarch's council members.

**Jessica** – Faerie with a southern accent, calls Lisa her sister.

**Jordan** – Early leader of the Daemoni who sought power over all, inadvertently helping to create the Amadis (read his story in *Genesis: A Soul Savers Novella*).

**Julia Acerbi** – Vampire and Amadis matriarch's council member. She'd been one of Rina's closest advisors and friends.

**Kali** – Daemoni sorceress who took over Martin Allbright's body. Dead.

**Katerina "Rina" Ames** – Past matriarch of the Amadis. Known abilities included telepathy, super strength and speed, flashing, bonding souls, converting souls to Amadis, making ballgowns everyday attire. Ascended.

**Kristen** – Human girl who started the London branch of AK's Angels with her sister, Ammi.

**Kuckaroo** – Amadis village in Australia.

**Lesley** – Daemoni vampire. Companion of Sonya and Alys. Died in the war.

**Lilith** – Bree's daughter and Tristan's sister. Dead.

**Lisa** – Faerie with a southern accent, calls Jessica her sister.

**Loft, The** – Formerly The Prepper's Stash House, a massive underground nuclear bunker that had been the storehouse for the multimillion dollar doomsday prep and survival training company. Given to the Amadis by Brogan, the owner, after A.K. Angels arrived for shelter and converted him. Sarcastically renamed The Loft.

**Lucas** – Alexis's sperm donor and leader of the Daemoni. Often (but not always) uses the last name Emerson.

**Lykora** – An Angelic being that is extremely loyal and highly protective of its master. When in hidden form, looks like a small white dog, but when in defensive mode, can grow as large as necessary to protect, has a wolf head and body, tiger stripes on a white coat, and feathered wings.

**Mages** – The wide classification of supernatural beings that can wield magic, including witches/wizards, warlocks, and Sorcerers/sorceresses. These general sub-classifications are based on strength of power. Some may call themselves by other names, depending on the type of magic they use, preference, or other reasons (e.g., Shamans, Druids, etc.).

**Martin Allbright** – Powerful warlock, Charlotte's husband and Owen's father.

**Merrick** – Sorcerer who tortured Alexis and Owen to learn the secret about the stones that control the Norman soldiers. Jeana's mate. Dead.

**Minh** – Vietnamese witch, member of the matriarch's council, oversees the Asian region.

**Miguel** - Human who traveled from Brazil after the war, Dani's papa.

**Molita** – Daemoni born warlock converted to Amadis during the war.

**Noah** – Sophia's twin brother, Rina's son, a Summoned son with the Daemoni and controlled by Kali.

**Norms/Normans** – Normal humans.

**Oliver Winston Chambers** – Sophia's true love who was turned to a vampire then buried under a building in Charlotte, North Carolina, for a century. Dead again.

**Ophelia** – Witch who serves as head of staff at the Amadis matriarch's mansion.

**Otherworld** – Currently unknown but seems to refer to Heaven and Hell, as well as Faerie.

**Owen Allbright** – Warlock and Alexis's so-called protector. Also like a brother to her and Tristan's best friend. Known abilities include shielding, cloaking, magical bindings, flashing, and pushing everyone's limits.

**Phillip Jones** – Human wife beater, child abuser, and overall scum of the earth who drove an older orange Camaro. Heather and Sonya's father. Dead.

**Pixies** - A type of fae; small, spits pixie dust that can be toxic to those of the Earthly realm.

**Portals** – Magical doorways that can only be created and controlled by sorcerers/sorceresses and extremely powerful warlocks like Owen. They allow teleportation to anywhere in the world just by stepping through.

**Ranker** - (Former) mayor of Misery's Edge who tried to arrest Alexis for murder.

**Rene** – Daemoni were-cheetah who chases Alexis down in Hades.

**Safe House** – Homes, lodges, and other accommodations scattered around the world where Amadis can retreat to when under attack or when going through the conversion or transformation process.

**Sasha** – Dorian's lykora, now loyal to the twins.

**Satan** – No explanation necessary.

**Savio** – Italian were-shark who was on Rina's council and was anti-Tristan.

**Scout** - Mayor of Misery's Edge.

**Seth** – Tristan's former name when he was Daemoni. The Daemoni still call him that.

**Shamara** - A Major Demon who's taken control of Misery's Edge.

**Sheree** – An Amadis were-tiger who'd been bitten and turned against her will by the Daemoni. She was Alexis's first ever conversion from Daemoni to Amadis. Now she helps with conversions of others and is a close friend to Alexis.

**Shield** – A magic spell performed by mages that puts a protective barrier around its subject. If the subject is not also cloaked, the subject can still be seen, so it's often used in conjunction with a cloaking spell.

**Shihab** – Wizard from Arabia who sat on Rina's council.

**Solomon** – Vampire, Katerina's partner, and Amadis council member. Known abilities include being scary AF. Dead.

**Sonya** – Recently turned vampire, now converted to Amadis. Heather's sister. A.K. Emerson's "biggest fan" (a/k/a stalker).

**Sophia Ames (a/k/a Mom a/k/a Mimi)** – Alexis's mother and Amadis daughter. Known abilities included telekinesis, summoning and manipulating water, persuading others to do as she likes, sensing the truth of a situation, super strength and speed, flashing, converting souls to Amadis. Ascended.

**Sorcerers/Sorceresses** – The most powerful of the mages that can boost their energy by siphoning more from the earth and everything around them. Their greed for power, narcissism, and general disdain for pretty much everyone make them loners and also not part of the Amadis.

**Stacey** – A faerie in England who helps Alexis and Tristan from time to time. Cohorts with Debbie.

**Stefan** – Warlock, council member, and Sophia's former protector. Known abilities included creating a protective shield, flashing, serving as Alexis's only father figure. Dead.

**Summoned Sons** – Amadis sons, twins of Amadis daughters/matriarchs, who always go to the Daemoni, as though magically summoned. Include Noah, Edmund, and Dorian.

**Sundae** – Alpha of the Georgia wolf pack. Trevor's mate.

**Sylvie (Aunt Sylvie)** – Blossom's aunt and leader of the Daytona Beach witch coven.

**Teah & Teal** – Human cousins who'd joined A.K.'s Angels in Florida with Heather and Sonya. Teachers at the school in The Loft.

**Trevor** – Amadis werewolf and leader of the main Florida wolf pack. Sundae's mate.

**Tristan Knight** – Former Daemoni converted to Amadis by Sophia. Matriarch's second, best friend, and husband. Dorian's dad. Sexy AF warrior. Known abilities include shooting fire from his palm, quickly determining the best solution if he knows enough of the facts, telekinesis, paralysis, instant killing power, super-duper strength and speed, brooding with guilt, giving a girl multiple Os.

**Vampires** – Supernatural beings that are sustained by blood. They can also feed on fear and other emotional energy. There are vampires on both the Amadis and the Daemoni sides.

**Vanessa** – Formerly one of the Daemoni's star vampires recently converted to Amadis. Alexis's half-sister, Victor's twin, and Lucas's daughter. Known abilities include stirring up trouble and pissing everyone off.

**Veil** – The magical barrier between the Earthly realm and the Otherworld. Beings in the Otherworld can often see through the Veil to the other side, but those on Earth cannot see into the Otherworld. Well, except for those with the sight, but the talent is very rare.

**Victor** – Vanessa's twin brother, Alexis's half-brother, Lucas's son and Daemoni vampire who's not too bright.

**Warlocks** – Part of the mage classification, supernatural beings who are born with the ability to wield magic and physically endowed with strength and speed, making them excellent warriors. They are not gender specific and are on both the Amadis and Daemoni sides.

**Whitby Abbey** – Ancient abbey on the northeastern coast of England. The place where Dorian was found, where Alexis faced off with Lucas, and where Sophia, Rina, and Winston died.

**Witches/Wizards** – Part of the mage classification, supernatural beings who are born with the ability to wield magic, usually using a wand as well as spells, incantations, potions, elemental energy, etc. While they can be quite powerful, their powers and physical strengths aren't as strong as Warlocks or Sorcerers. Using the term Witch or Wizard was traditionally by gender, but really is up to each individual's preference. There are Witches and Wizards on both the Amadis and Daemoni sides.

**Were-creatures/animals (a/k/a Shifters)** – Supernatural beings with two combined spirits—human and animal—and they can physically shift between their two forms. There is a were-creature/shifter for nearly every predatory species on Earth, and they're on both the Amadis and the Daemoni sides.

**Zombies** – Reanimated corpses with deadly bites. Created by mixing necromancy magic with fatal and highly contagious viruses, such as Ebola. Lucas made them as an experiment and to provide meatsuits for the Demons he planned to let loose on Earth.

# ABOUT THE AUTHOR

Kristie Cook is a lifelong, award-winning writer in various genres, primarily New Adult paranormal romance and contemporary fantasy. Her internationally bestselling, award-winning Soul Savers Series includes seven books, as well as several companion novellas and short stories. Over 1.2 million Soul Savers books have been downloaded. She has also written The Book of Phoenix trilogy, a New Adult paranormal romance series. Her books have been featured in *USA Today's* HEA section, on Good Morning America, and in the Emmy's Gifting Suite.

Kristie also created, writes in, and publishes the award-winning Havenwood Falls shared world, a collaborative project with multiple series, dozens of authors, and countless stories.

Besides writing, Kristie enjoys reading, cooking, traveling, getting her hippie on, and feeding her addictions to coffee, chocolate, cheese, and her latest TV obsession. She has lived in eleven states, but currently calls Florida home.

# CONNECT WITH ME ONLINE

I love to hear from and connect with readers. Please don't be shy.

Facebook Reader Group: https://www.facebook.com/groups/ClubKC. KristieCook

Email: kristie@kristiecook.com

Author's Website & Blog: http://www.KristieCook.com

Facebook: http://www.facebook.com/AuthorKristieCook

Goodreads: https://www.goodreads.com/KristieCook

Instagram: http://instagram.com/kristiecookauth

BookBub: https://www.bookbub.com/authors/kristie-cook

*Word of mouth is very important for any author. If you enjoyed the book, please consider leaving a review, even if it's only a sentence or two. This is one of the most important and appreciated things you can do for an author.*

# ACKNOWLEDGMENTS

Gratitude first goes to my Creator, my eternal Source of life, love, and creativity—and everything else.

Much love and appreciation to my family, particularly to Terry, Keena, and Peggi, who believe so fully in me and my special form of magic.

Huge thanks to Stacey Nixon, Heather Wakefield, and Kim Myers for your feedback and eagle eyes. I love your reactions to that ending.

To my readers who have stuck with me through these ten books and through all the others I've written, a ginormous thank you. You are why I publish! I may always be a writer to make my soul happy, but you make it worth all the extra work, heartache, fears, and stress to hit that publish button and put my stories out into the world. It's been so much fun continuing this series, and I can't wait for you to read what comes next.

I love you all—until the end of forever and always.

# BOOKS BY KRISTIE COOK

**SOUL SAVERS**

Recommended Reading Order:

A Demon's Promise

An Angel's Purpose

Genesis: A Soul Savers Novella

Dangerous Devotion

Dark Power

Sacred Wrath

Unholy Torment

Fractured Faith

Age of Angels Part I: Awakened

Age of Angels Part II: Lost

Age of Angels Part III: Marked

Prophecy of the Wolves: (A Soul Savers Tie-In Novella)

Wonder: A Soul Savers Collection of Holiday Short Stories & Recipes

**KNIGHTS OF SOULS AND SHADOWS**

Knights of Souls and Shadows, Book 1

**HAVENWOOD FALLS**

Recommended Reading Order:

Forget You Not

Lose You Not

Break Me Not

The Collector: Awakening

Savage Salvation (Sin & Silk)

Sun & Moon Academy Book One: Fall Semester
Sun & Moon Academy Book Two: Fall Semester

The Winged & the Wicked (with T.V. Hahn)
Havenwood Falls Short Story Anthology 2018
Havenwood Falls Short Story Anthology 2019
Havenwood Falls Short Story Anthology 2020

### BOOK OF PHOENIX
The Space Between
The Space Beyond
The Space Within

www.ingramcontent.com/pod-product-compliance
Lightning Source LLC
Chambersburg PA
CBHW020740130626
46554CB00006B/2075